LONG SHOT

Adam Keel had only one dream left: to breed a strain of longhorns that no longer had Texas tick-fever in their blood. Then Shelby McMann came into his life. McMann could not bend Adam Keel to his will, so he got him five years on a brutal chain gang. That would bring Keel to his senses, he reckoned. But he was wrong. The mysterious Warbonnets rang to the crash of sixguns and the dying screams of McMann's men, until finally there was only McMann left — and Adam Keel.

Books by Tyler Hatch
in the Linford Western Library:

A LAND TO DIE FOR
BUCKSKIN GIRL
DEATHWATCH TRAIL

TYLER HATCH

$\blacklozenge$

LONG SHOT

Complete and Unabridged

LINFORD
Leicester

First published in Great Britain in 2000 by
Robert Hale Limited
London

First Linford Edition
published 2001
by arrangement with
Robert Hale Limited
London

British Library CIP Data

Hatch, Tyler
  Long shot.—Large print ed.—
  Linford western library
  1. Western stories
  2. Large type books
  I. Title
  823.9'14 [F]

  ISBN 0–7089–4579–1

Published by
F. A. Thorpe (Publishing)
Anstey, Leicestershire

Set by Words & Graphics Ltd.
Anstey, Leicestershire
Printed and bound in Great Britain by
T. J. International Ltd., Padstow, Cornwall

This book is printed on acid-free paper

1

Alone!

He had been on the run for three days before he realized that the men hunting him were using an Indian tracker.

Not just any Indian, it had to be the Mescalero. The one they called *Copperhead*, after the snake, because the man was silent and deadly.

No wonder their dust cloud had been between him and the horizon every damn time he looked! Someone must have gotten smart enough to know they would need more than normal tracking expertise to run him to ground.

And the Mescalero hated his guts into the bargain.

Well, there was only one thing to do if he hoped to get out of this with a whole skin.

He had to kill the Indian. There was

no other way of beating the Mescalero.

It would be no easy chore at any time, but now his only weapon was a stone knife and crude bow and a handful of flint-tipped arrows. Which meant, with the poor cast of the bow itself, he would have to get mighty close and make that first shot count, drive the flint head deep into the Mescalero's foul heart. Even then most likely he would have to pin him with two or three other arrows before he died: he had the resilient toughness of a grizzly.

Weak from lack of decent food and water and rest, it was going to be one hell of a chore, one he hadn't counted on. All he'd figured on doing was outrunning the posse in the Warbonnets — and that would be chore enough even if he was well fed and in good shape. Still, he could do it, and he would: no one knew these mountains like he did.

Except, maybe, the goddamn Mescalero!

Sheriff Cole knew that; McMann

wouldn't, but he'd be more than willing to be guided by Cole — or even Joel Askins, who knew a little more about him than most. The thing was, he had the problem to solve and the longer he took to do it, the closer Copperhead would get to him. With McMann and his killers right behind.

All right. As always, he needed to find water first. He could handle an empty belly a little while longer, but water had priority.

He snapped his head up at the sudden busy chirping of birds. He was holed-up in the adobe ruins of the old stageline swing-station at Morgan's Leap. Now he saw a pair of swallows swooping in out of the gathering dusk, hovering in the corner made by rotting beams and crumbling adobe. *They were building a nest!* And, as always, in *mud!* Little pellets of it held in their small beaks. *Damp mud!*

That meant they were getting it at a source within easy flight distance. He

3

waited until they had placed the mud pellets the way they wanted, watched them turn, still chattering, and swoop away on a flight-path to the south-west.

He stood cautiously, watching the distant Mescalero as he hunkered down, studying the ground for man-tracks where the brushline ended and the hard red earth of the slopes began. It would take Copperhead at least another hour before he found anything — if at all — and by then it would be too dark to continue.

He deliberately scraped some grass fibres from the sandals he had woven for his feet, leaving the few dry strands for the Indian to find. He took a wide swing out to the south-west line, crumbled a few more strands, giving the Mescalero direction. Then he set off through the rocks and draws, following the general direction of the swallows' flight . . .

He was at the water-hole by dark. It was not much more than a mud puddle, but birds and animals had

4

gathered for their nightly fill. He was tempted to send a shaft through a small javelina but didn't want to make it *that* easy for Copperhead: it would only make the man more wary if he found signs of food having been successfully taken.

But he was able to slake his thirst in time, without spooking the wildlife, and his belly growled hungrily, sagging against his spine as he chose his ambush site and settled down to wait . . .

Thinking about how he came to be here, waiting in hiding beside a muddy pool, half-starved, still wearing ragged butternut-brown prison clothes, waiting to kill a man — one who would try his best to kill him first if he got the chance . . .

*　　*　　*

It was early morning and the dust haze over the San Antonio cattle yards, a mile from town at track's-end of the

5

railroad, was golden in the slanted sunlight.

And Adam Keel was having a heap more trouble than he had expected with his newly arrived Hereford seed bull. The damn beast was twice as big as the agent had led him to believe and somehow on the journey down from Dallas the brass ring through the bull's nose had been torn out. Now blood and froth mixed to dribble from his nostrils, giving the animal a mighty mean look.

And the Hereford was mean, damn mean, as Keel learned when he stepped between the rails into the pen, assured by the smirking yard-handlers that the bull was a real pussycat. Within seconds of entering, Keel was running for the fence, leaping wildly for the highest rail. Even then the bull slammed into the lodgepole timbers with enough force to dislodge the man and Keel tumbled in a heap on the outside. The bull pawed and snorted, covering him with dirt. He sat up spitting, wiping grit from his dark frontier moustache.

Renny and Art, the yardmen, guffawed, Renny saying, 'That was the *goddamned* neatest ass-over I ever did see!'

Keel smiled crookedly, took his coil of rope and climbed back on the rails. It was the bull's nose that made him so ornery, Keel decided, glancing at a Mexican kid staring wide-eyed between the fence bars.

'Hey, *muchacho*, want a nickel?'

'*Si, señor!*' the kid said eagerly, running up and holding out a grubby hand.

Keel smiled faintly as he shook his head. 'You go fetch Doc Delassandro — the vet. You know, animal doctor?'

'*Si*, I know 'im, *señor*. I bring 'im and you pay, eh?'

'Now you got it . . . '

The kid set off in the direction of town and some of the handlers started joshing the dusty rancher again but Keel paid little attention, wondering how much it was going to cost him to have the vet do something about the bull's torn nostrils.

'Mr McMann wants to see you, feller.'

Keel heard the voice close by as he straddled the top bar, looked down and saw a hard-eyed, lean-as-a-rail *hombre* standing there looking up at him. Immediately, Adam Keel noticed that the man's clothes were store-bought and of decent quality. And maybe there was something vaguely familiar about him, too.

'You speaking to me?' he asked.

'If your name's Keel, I am.'

'I'm Keel. But I don't know no one named McMann.'

'You don't have to know him — don't change a thing. He still wants to see *you*.' The man jerked a thumb over one shoulder, keeping his left hand close to the butt of the single six-gun he wore on a concha-studded cartridge belt.

Keel lifted his gaze, saw the big, varnished Pullman rail car on the siding nearest the depot, parked away from the dust of the cow yards.

'McMann's in *that*?' asked Keel.

The lean man curled a lip. 'He *owns* it, for God's sake! It's *Shelby* McMann I'm talking about. He owns the railroad and about half of Texas, not to mention a fair slice of Colorado.'

'I've heard of him,' admitted Keel. 'Still don't know him — and I'm busy right now.'

The lean man's face hardened, his hollow cheeks burning slightly at the rebuff. His left hand tightened its grip on the gun butt. 'Feller, I was told to ask politely: I done that — now, you come see Mr McMann — *pronto!*' The six-gun appeared in his fist instantly and the cowhands who had been watching suddenly found chores to do across the other side of the pen.

The gun barrel jerked impatiently, and Keel, sober-faced, swung a leg over the top rail and climbed on down. The lean man reached out to shove his shoulder and Keel slapped the arm aside with the rope, swung the coil back and took the startled hardcase across the side of the head. The man staggered, tried to keep his footing but had his legs kicked out from under him and sprawled in the dust. Keel's boot pinned his hand and gun to the ground and the rancher leaned down, wrenched the Colt free and stepped back. The lean man got slowly to his feet, eyes blazing, shaking his bruised hand.

'Gimme me that gun, you son of a bitch!'

'You not only need a lesson in tact, mister, but you got breath like a grizzly's armpit,' Keel said and gunwhipped the man suddenly. He crumpled to the ground, hitting his head on the rails on the way down. Keel stooped, grabbed a leg and pulled him out from under the bottom rail, then tossed his gun into the nearby water trough.

By that time, the Mexican kid was back with the huffing and puffing Doc Dellasandro.

Keel flipped the grinning kid a nickel and as the vet mopped his doughy face, the man groaned. 'Don't tell me — the damn bull's crankier than a bear that's sat on a wasp — and all because of that torn septum!' He set mournful eyes on Adam Keel. 'Christ, Adam, couldn't you've found me something simpler? That bull's ready to tear up the countryside!'

'How much to treat him, Doc? And I want to get back to the spread soon as I can. Old Stew's out there alone and his sight's failing by the day.'

Dellasandro heaved a sigh. 'Well, I'm going to have to knock him out, clean up his nostrils and likely his throat, too, before I even start sewing . . . I was you, I wouldn't count on leaving town before tomorrow.'

Keel swore softly but nodded. 'Do what you got to, Doc. Just don't charge too much; I've had an expensive month . . . '

The vet grunted, working over the big black leather bag he had brought with him. He took out a large hypodermic with a thick needle and began to fill the syringe from a dark brown bottle. He glanced up at the curious yard handlers now gathering around.

'We'll need a hand to subdue the Hereford, boys. How many volunteers have we got . . . ?'

They disbanded so fast Keel wondered if they had actually been there. He went after them and managed to persuade two, including Renny the jokester, to lend a hand. Then it was all dust and sweat and a little blood and torn hide as they ganged-up on the snorting bull, roped its hind legs first, almost hernia-ed themselves trying to pull the legs out from under. Finally, they managed it and the bull went down and then Doc Dellasandro ran in with the syringe tied to a long slat of wood he had picked up during the struggle to catch the Hereford. It plunged home and the bull bellowed and convulsed, a horn ripping Renny's old trousers near the groin. He shrieked and the other yarder and Keel grinned.

'I think I missed that, Renny,' Keel said. 'You want to do it again for me.'

Renny was whitefaced. 'Judas, man, I almost lost my *cojones*, not to mention my pecker. Ain't nothin' to joke about!'

'Spoil-sport,' said Keel winking.

'You're a hard man, Mr Keel. And a violent one.'

The rancher glanced up at the sound of the mellow voice, straightened quickly when he saw the man he had gunwhipped standing unsteadily, holding a wet kerchief against his swollen head. Beside him stood a medium-sized man in a truly beautiful pearl-grey broadcloth suit. A diamond or some kind of jewel winked in the hot Texas sun in the gold stickpin in his silk cravat. His flesh was firm and tanned, glossy with health and good eating. His eyes were grey, almost the same colour as his suit and what hair showed beneath his flat-crowned hat was black and curly. Keel figured him to be pushing fifty. He leaned on a gold-handled cane and there was a ring with a red stone on his little finger. Slightly behind him stood a third man, tall as Keel himself and as broad of shoulder. His axeblade face was sober and he would have been fairly good looking except for the size of his nose. Not only was it too large, but it had been broken at some time and set over to the left, above a thin-lipped mouth. Cold, blue eyes stared hard at Keel and then the man nodded, stepping clear of the man in the grey suit so that Keel could see the twin six-guns in the plain, though oiled, leather holsters.

'Been a few years, Adam,' the man said quietly.

Keel nodded, looking somehow wary now. 'Joel Askins — wondered what had happened to you.'

'I haven't been hiding like you, if that's what you mean. I've been working for Mr McMann — I kind of see that he gets what he wants.'

Keel nodded, smiling faintly. 'Like getting to see me.'

'Yeah, like that . . . ' Askins gestured

to the gunwhipped man. 'Bruno here didn't ask you nice enough, it seems.'

Keel looked at McMann who nodded civilly and thrust out his right hand. 'Shelby McMann, Mr Keel. Don't mind if I call you 'Adam', do you? I feel as if I know you. Joel has told me quite a lot and folk in San Antone added to it . . . Seems you're quite a talented man.'

Keel said nothing, waiting.

There was maybe a slight flicker in McMann's eyes now. 'You run a ranch where no one else has been successful in the past and I hear tell you're about to try some innovative breeding.'

'Just an idea I have,' Keel said slowly. He scratched at his dusty frontier moustache, watching McMann warily. There was something about this well-fed *hombre* . . .

McMann gestured to the now sleeping bull as the vet prepared him for the surgery. 'Longhorns aren't good beef cattle, you know. Too lean, meat's too tough, they carry tick-fever. Crossing Herefords with them has been tried before, same as with Devon and Durham. None of 'em were successful.'

'Because those men expected instant results. You can't breed-out Texas tick-fever in one generation of long-horns. It's going to take time.'

'Well, perhaps it has possibilities in that case. But such a venture will mean some lean times, Adam, while awaiting results. Perhaps I can help financially.'

'You want to back me?' asked Keel sharply.

'Not back you, no. But I need you to do a small job for me, and I can pay well enough to help your project along.'

'Never thought of it in those terms,' drawled Keel. 'It's just a dream I'd like to see come true.'

'You have to face up to the possibility of failure,' McMann told him flatly. 'Prepare for it. Come on back to my Pullman where we can talk in comfort and privacy over a cool drink . . . agreed?'

McMann took Keel by the right elbow and his smile faded as the rancher pulled free immediately and stepped back. McMann was startled and Askins dropped a hand to a gun butt then smiled faintly, shaking his head at Keel.

'You ain't changed a lot, Adam. Still kind of touchy, ain't you?' Askins spoke to McMann even while still watching Keel. 'Sorry, boss, should've warned you: never touch Adam's gun arm or cramp him on that side.'

McMann was sober now, his eyes bleak. He obviously wasn't used to anyone resisting his wishes. 'A mistake on my part then — I apologize, Mr Keel. Let's seal it with a draught of some fine malt whisky I import from Scotland . . .'

Keel didn't move. 'Sorry, Mr McMann. I'm busy. My bull needs attention and I can keep my bills down if I help the doc . . .'

'Good God, man, I can — *Don't turn your back on me when I'm talking to you!*'

Keel started, stopped his turn away

and looked back at the man in the grey suit. The gold-headed cane was up and pointing at him. And he saw the hole in the base, the glint of blued metal an inch or so inside the gold ferrule on the end.

It was a gun stick and, at that moment, pointing directly at his heart.

Keel slapped it out of McMann's hand with his coil of rope, nodded to Askins, then ducked between the pen rails to go help Doc Dellasandro. McMann stood incredulous.

Keel was busy with the vet for a time and when he looked over his shoulder, McMann and his men were no longer in sight.

'Thought he'd never take the hint,' he quipped to the bloody-handed vet as the man tied off the last suture in the Hereford's tender septum.

The bull was beginning to stir groggily as the vet wiped his hands and said, 'Watch your back, Adam. He's a mean one, mighty mean.'

2

Crowd Him!

'He's the toughest man I've ever known, boss,' Joel Askins told McMann back inside the elaborately fitted out Pullman car. 'We rode together on the border one time.'

McMann had brought his own chef with him, and his mistress, a young chestnut-haired beauty by the name of Della Lorrance. She dressed in the finest clothes, ate the best food alongside McMann and drank the best wines. She had everything of the best and what she had to do to earn it was no problem to Della Lorrance. She knew her limitations. She wasn't very smart, intelligence-wise, but she did have a good memory and she could hold her own in any conversation with anyone from a congressman to a cowhand. She prided herself on that and McMann showed her off with his own brand of pride when it suited him. And she sure knew how to please a man . . .

Right now, she was sitting on an ornate button-down sofa McMann had imported from Paris, long legs curled under her crinoline skirts as she leafed through a book with a gold-embossed leather binding. She showed no interest in Askins' conversation with McMann who seemed kind of tight around the lips. That was why she looked at him surreptitiously from time to time: it was important to always gauge his moods: they tended to be unpredictable and stormy.

'Specially when he didn't get his own way — which was not very often — but right now someone named Keel seemed to have him stymied and riding the edge of a cyclonic mood.

'I don't care how tough he is,' McMann now said in answer to Askins. 'I want him to do that job for me and I *always* get what I want, you know that. Where is he now?'

'Bruno said he went to one of the saloons with a couple of the yardmen.'

'Send someone down and ask him nicely once more to come see me — tell him to come for supper. Andre is cooking some French thing that might put him in a more compliant mood.'

Askins looked a bit sceptical, but nodded, went out and hunted up Bruno Penn, giving him his orders.

The man's face still looked lopsided from the gunwhipping and he touched the bruised swelling gently. 'I'll ask him — and I hope he refuses.'

'None of that! The boss said just ask. You do more than that and I'll give you a knot on the other side of your head.'

Penn went out scowling, hitching at his left-hand-slung Colt, pausing in the dusk to check the cylinder. There was still a chance this Keel might provoke him into a gunfight. He could always hope.

But maybe it was the two beers and

the whiskey chaser Keel had consumed that made him more mellow, for when Bruno extended McMann's invitation, adding that it was genuine French food being offered, Keel glanced at Art and Renny and winked.

'Got to be better than the slop they serve in Pancho's diner. See you later fellers. Maybe I'll bring you a frog's leg.'

'I know a place you could put that!' Renny replied with a grin.

★ ★ ★

It was an enjoyable meal and Keel also enjoyed meeting Della Lorrance. He had never been this close to such a beautiful and well-dressed woman before, but none of it showed on his face. He was polite when asked questions, volunteered nothing.

Not that he had much chance: McMann monopolized the conversation, detailing his assets — a railroad, huge cattle ranches in Montana, an interest in a weapons and munitions factory in Minnesota, some overseas 'interests' — not specified — vast tracts of land in Texas.

'And when you get right down to it, I inherited most of my money from a distant cousin who was some sort of earl or duke in Ireland where my ancestors came from. Rich by right!'

'Glad I don't have the worry of taking care of all that money,' Keel replied and McMann was momentarily stunned, then smiled thinly.

'Keeps me on my toes. But I *make* time to do the things I want.' He gestured to one wall behind him in the dining-saloon. It contained a few mounted animal heads and several ornately carved oak gun racks. One of the guns had been nickel-plated and blazed in the light of the oil lamps.

'Hunting is my main interest outside of my business, Adam,' McMann went on. 'Hunting — and long-range target shooting.' He signalled Askins who was standing in the curtained doorway and the bodyguard took down a heavy-looking gun that reminded Keel vaguely of a Sharps buffalo rifle, except as far as he could see it had no hammer. 'How d'you like that one, Adam?'

Keel took the gun, aware of the girl's cool gaze, hefted it, worked the lever action, flipped up the peep-sight. 'Fine gun — I see it's built on a Sharps' action but I've never seen one like this before.'

McMann chuckled, pleased. 'And you won't — custom made. A Sharps-Borchadt. Built on a Sharps action but with an internal firing pin in the breech. Smooth and efficient.' He paused for effect. 'Efficient enough for me to lead the American winning team at the '77 Creedmoor shoot against a bunch of rash Irishmen who issued the challenge.'

Keel was impressed despite himself. McMann made some sort of sign with his head and eyes and Askins put the gun back and while McMann boasted about the grizzly and Canadian moose he had shot with the rifle 'at one mile distance', the bodyguard took down the nickel-plated rifle and handed it to Keel.

It was a Remington custom-made Creedmoor target gun, the kind that Nelson Story and his trailherders had blooded along the Bozeman Trail against Chief Red Cloud, but refined and beautifully built. The rolling-block action made hardly any sound at all.

'Real elegant — but any game'd be gone over the horizon once the sun flashed off the nickel finish.'

McMann scowled and then gave a brief chuckle, saying, 'My favourite weapon.' He smiled proudly. 'I've knocked a mustang clean off his feet with a bullet from that gun . . . ' He paused again, looking expectantly into Keel's wolfish face. 'At a distance officially measured at one mile, one hundred and ten yards, two feet and three inches! So reflection isn't important after all . . . '

The saloon was silent and Keel looked up, suddenly aware that he was

25

expected to enthuse over this, or at least show how impressed he was. Instead, he said, 'Why would you want to shoot a mustang, for Chris'sakes?'

McMann's face coloured and he tapped his manicured fingers against the Irish linen cloth. He spoke between his teeth. 'Because — it — was — *there*!'

Then he gave that short laugh again, looked around the room and Askins dutifully smiled and the girl stretched her full red lips in a token effort. Keel shrugged, handed the gun back to Joel Askins.

'Well, it sure ain't any sporting rifle.'

McMann leaned forward across the polished table, his face mask-like now. 'You're missing the point, Adam! The *distance*, man! Over a mile! And I can hit consistently at that range. You must admit that's quite an accomplishment.'

'If you see any fun in it, I guess it is. That rifle got something to do with why you wanted to see me?'

It took McMann a moment or two to

bottle up the rising anger but then he forced a tight smile.

'I see you are a perceptive man, too, Adam — yes. I understand you know the Warbonnet Hills to the south and west of here better than any man living.' He paused but Keel said nothing. 'Very well, we take that as read. I am a man who has shot many trophy animals, only a very few you see here on my wall. But the games room in my house back in Colorado is crammed with all kinds of animals — not just American and Mexican. I have shot African elephant and rhino, lion, buffalo and even the elusive leopard . . . but I have only managed to kill a mediocre cougar — '

'They show some sense and stay out of the way, mostly,' commented Keel.

McMann nodded impatiently, not appreciating the interruption. 'But there is a legend of a giant mountain cat in the Warbonnets — and added to the legend is the story that you have actually seen this animal!'

Keel stared back at the man, flicked his gaze to the girl who was trying to look interested, but underneath he figured she was bored. 'I have. I shot at it, think I might've flicked an inch or two of hair off his shoulders . . . '

'Aimed too high,' dropped in McMann, his eyes alight now.

Keel shook his head. 'No. I'd taken a fall, busted an ankle and was jammed in the rocks when he showed up on a ledge above me, silhouetted against the sun. He was coming down to drink at the waterhole where I'd fallen. He snarled at me and I fired my Colt, my rifle being jammed somewhere under me. Bullet ricocheted across his back. He flinched and I saw those yellow eyes look straight at me. Then for no reason I've been able to figure, he just turned, dropped down off the ledge and drank at the water-hole and disappeared into the dusk.'

McMann reared back in his chair. 'You let him escape!'

'I wasn't trying to kill him; I just

wanted him out of there. Sure, I'd've tried to nail him if he'd charged, but he didn't.' Keel's voice hardened. 'That's why I'll never hunt him. He didn't have to let me live, not the size he is.'

'You owe him a debt,' the girl said suddenly in her quiet voice. 'And you intend to pay it.'

McMann glared at her. 'Go paint your face or something, Della! This is man talk.'

She shrugged, stood, nodded to Keel and made for the curtained doorway where Askins pulled the drapes aside for her.

'She's right,' Keel said, standing suddenly. 'I figure I owe that cat my life . . . That was an elegant meal, McMann. Obliged. But I best go get some sleep. I've a long way to drive my bull tomorrow.'

McMann stood quickly. 'Wait! You haven't heard my offer . . . I'll pay you five hundred dollars to guide me into those hills so I can hunt down that giant cat!'

'You won't hunt down anything using that Remington or the Sharps . . . all you'll do is have me flush the cat out on to some ridge a mile away from your camp and you'll lie back in your chair and take your shot. Not interested, but thanks all the same.'

He started for the door, Askins quickly stepping between him and the exit. Keel stopped, looked steadily at the bodyguard.

'Step aside, Joel,' he said quietly, but then McMann was beside him, holding him by the left elbow.

'A thousand dollars! You'll be able to buy more seed bulls, a better class of heifer for your breeding programme. What d'you say to that, Adam?'

'Same as I said before — thanks, but no thanks.'

He shouldered Askins aside. The bodyguard was obviously awaiting orders from McMann but the man only glared.

As Keel stepped out into the night and down to the cinders, McMann said, 'Adam — I don't think you quite understand. It is my intention to hunt down and kill that animal. I *always* get what I want. Save us all a lot of wasted time by thinking over my offer . . . '

Keel walked away into the night.

Askins closed the door gently. 'I can send a man after him to bring him back.'

McMann looked at him as if he didn't see him, then blinked. 'Yes, all right. Send a couple of men. But wait till he returns to his saloon — then they're to crowd him, hard. I want to see if Adam Keel has as much guts and integrity as he would have us believe . . . '

★ ★ ★

Keel recognized Bruno Penn, of course, as he drank one final drink before starting up the stairs towards his room. There was another man with him, bigger, more brutal looking. They saw him and hurried up the stairs behind him. He turned at the top, waiting.

Penn and the big man paused a few steps from the landing. 'McMann don't take 'no' for an answer when he really wants somethin',' growled Bruno.

'This time he will.'

Keel started to turn and the big man leapt up, reaching for the tall man's shoulder. As soon as his fingers touched Keel, the rancher spun about fast, sank a fist into the big one's midriff, gripped his belt and with the other hand, grabbed for his throat. The big man was gagging for breath as his air was cut off and Keel swung him effortlessly into Bruno and the pair clattered and somersaulted down the stairs to lie in a tangled, dazed heap at the bottom.

Keel was surprised to see Sheriff Andy Cole walk out of the staring crowd. He stood four-square solid, looking down at Penn and his hardcase companion before lifting his eyes to Keel at the top of the stairs.

Cole looked tough, saying, 'You ain't cuttin' loose the wolf in my town tonight, Keel! I told you last time was the last time!'

'Relax, Sheriff. I tried to save the big feller when he lost his balance on the top step, is all. When he fell he took the other one with him.'

Cole sneered, 'I know how mean you can be, Keel! We all know. Now you watch your step. Mr McMann has had a talk with me earlier and he can do a lot for this town — couple of spur tracks out to the ranches, a freight line clear down to Laredo. He can make a lot of work for folk around here.'

The lawman had the attention of the men in the bar now. Most of them sensed that Keel was somehow involved in what Cole was saying and they crowded closer.

'He'll make a dollar or two out of it, I don't doubt,' Keel said, starting to turn away.

'All depends on how much co-operation he gets from folk around here.' He looked hard at Keel. '*Some* folk.'

Keel frowned. 'He wants that big cat that bad? He's saying that if I don't guide him into the Warbonnets, he'll run his spur tracks and freight line someplace else?'

The crowd murmured and Cole, sensing he had them behind him, for every one of them was seeing dollar-signs, said sharply, 'That's about it. Now, you've lived around here for quite a spell, Keel. This town's done plenty for you. Time to pay your debts.'

Keel shook his head slowly. 'McMann must have more money than brains. Or he's a downright liar.'

That didn't go down too well with the crowd, but Keel moved on down the dim passage to the room he had rented for the night. As he turned the key in the door, he heard animated talk starting up down in the bar.

That damn McMann! Keel suddenly realized that it wasn't that the man wanted to hunt the big cat so much: what he *really* wanted was to bend Keel to his will. He simply wouldn't

34

— couldn't — take no for an answer.

Well, lots of luck, Keel thought as he stepped inside.

★ ★ ★

Shelby McMann contemptuously flung a double-eagle at the feet of the battered hardcase called Mooney, the man who had been Bruno Penn's sidekick in the saloon.

'Get out!' McMann snapped. 'I don't employ losers!'

Mooney, sullen, his face still bleeding from being thrown down the saloon stairs, picked up the money and glared at McMann, seemed about to speak but stopped, looking towards Bruno. 'What about him? He got throwed down them stairs, too.'

Penn turned and hit the man with his gun barrel across the bridge of the nose. Mooney howled as Penn ran him to the door of the Pullman and heaved him out into the night.

'You're on your last chance, Bruno,'

McMann said coldly. 'Any more mistakes and you're finished here, too.'

'I won't make no more mistakes with Keel, boss.'

McMann waved him away, contemptuously, then saw Della Lorrance standing in the doorway in a nightdress mostly covered with a silk gown.

'Why don't you come to bed, Shell? You're upsetting yourself over nothing . . . Keel's a nobody.'

McMann's eyes blazed. 'A *nobody* who insulted me by refusing a genuine offer! *No one* throws my offers back in my face, let alone a *nobody*!' He strode forward swiftly, really enjoying the flare of alarm in the girl's eyes. 'And you're adding to that insult by telling me a *nobody* has defied me!'

'Shell, I only meant . . . '

He punched her brutally in the midriff and she gagged, her knees buckling, hands reaching instinctively towards him for support. He knocked them away, slapped her across the face, back and forth, took her smooth, slim shoulders between his hands and shook her, rapping her head twice against the doorframe.

Breathing hard he reached for her bosom and twisted painfully. He stepped back and she fell to her knees. When he turned, he saw Joel Askins standing impassively in the other doorway.

'Get her cleaned up — I've a job for her!'

3

Lonely Trail

Keel answered the door with a gun in his hand and the lamp on the bedside table turned down low. The room was full of shadows and, in his stockinged feet, stripped to the waist, preparing to go to bed, he inched the door back. There was still plenty of noise coming from the bar downstairs as he peered out into the dim passage.

Then the door slammed back against him and he took an involuntary step backwards as someone came quickly into the room. He caught a whiff of perfume, the rustle of fabric.

'Close it quickly! I mustn't be seen coming here!'

It was the girl — McMann's woman. *What was her name again?* Oh, yeah, Della someone-or-other.

He closed the door and held the gun half-way to waist level, thumb in the curve of the hammer, as he turned to face her. She looked just as beautiful as she had in the Pullman except — except her face bore the marks of having been beaten.

There were red marks on both cheeks that might turn to bruises; a swelling under the right eye; The full lips looked puffy. As she set down the carpetbag she was carrying, he saw her wince, grab at her lower left side.

He waited.

'I'm in trouble,' she said breathlessly. 'He beat me and — I — I've walked out on him. If he finds me he — he'll kill me.'

'Guess you mean McMann. So why come here?'

'You — You're the only one I could turn to. The only man I've ever seen defy McMann, insult him actually, and walk away in one piece.' She stepped towards him, grabbing at his arm. He eased her aside as it was his gun arm and she held his left above the elbow, looking up into his face. 'You've got to help me!'

'What can I do?' His voice was neutral and she took some comfort in the fact that it wasn't coldly dismissive.

'I — I don't know. I'm stranded. I haven't any money. Shell buys me almost anything I want but he never lets me have cash.'

'Just in case you're stupid enough to pull the kind of stunt you're pulling now, I guess.'

Her eyes blazed briefly, but then she nodded, lowering her gaze. 'I know it's stupid. It was just an impulse — but now . . . I daren't go back!'

'Well, what do you want from me?'

'Joel Askins says you have a ranch about fifteen miles out at a place called Anchor Basin . . . a lonely place, he said. Maybe I could stay a while? Just until Shell gets tired of looking for me and then . . . well, you could give me my train-fare to someplace . . . ' She lifted her eyes to him. 'I could . . . earn it, if you like . . . '

He knew what she was saying but his face didn't change expression. 'That's how you make a living, huh?'

Her face hardened and her eyes narrowed. 'Look, Keel, my main asset is my looks. I've had men chasing me since I was twelve years old. It didn't take me long to wake up to the fact that instead of giving myself to them for nothing, I could talk them into buying me nice things. I had no parents that I remember. I grew up in an orphanage, ran away, and — '

'You're breaking my heart.'

She swung at him but he parried easily. 'Damn you! It's true! OK, so I'm a whore, but it's the only way I know that'll give me the high style of living I've grown accustomed to.'

He was a mite surprised that she was so open about it and mentally put a tick against her name as something in her favour. 'Well, you'd sure be dropping down a lot of rungs on the ladder if you came to live at my place. I've got an oldster staying with me, feller who rescued me from some Indians who'd stolen me when I was a shaver . . . old Stew Ormond. He's going blind and he's none too careful about washing or going outside to relieve himself in the middle of the night. I try to keep things reasonable but . . . '

Her face showed her distaste but she made an effort to cover it. 'If it'll keep me away from McMann . . . '

'You're sure he'll come after you?'

'Of course! Maybe he won't want me any more, but no one walks out on Shelby McMann — except you.' Then she frowned and looked at him sharply. 'If you were — say you were to go to him and tell him all right, you'll guide him into the hills, that'd keep him away and he'd forget about me, or, at least, wouldn't bother about me while he's hunting. I could look after your old friend and perhaps slip away before you return.'

Keel said nothing.

She moved closer and he felt her

pelvis touch him as she traced her fingers across his white, muscular chest with its bullet and knife-fight scars. 'I could make it worth your while right now . . . I mean, if you went to him in the morning, that'd be soon enough . . . '

He took her by the arm, swung her around as he rammed his gun into his belt and opened the door. She staggered as he flung her into the passage and kicked her carpetbag after her. As she regained her balance, her eyes blazed at him.

'Now McMann's insulting me if he thinks I'd fall for a childish play like that — '

Her face straightened. 'Oh, don't do this, Keel! Don't throw me out and send me back to him! He doesn't tolerate people who don't do what he wants . . . '

She started towards him and he shook his head as he closed the door and propped a chair under the knob. She hammered on the panels for a while. whispering his name hoarsely. Then there was a blast of swearing that would have done credit to any mule-skinner, and he heard her heels tapping away down the hall towards the stairs.

There was anger building in him but he deliberately forced it down. I'm gonna have to do something about this McMann, he thought as he blew out the lamp and lay down on the bed. The son of a bitch is gonna be a pain in the butt.

Then glass shattered behind and to the left of the bed and he was rolling off, snatching his gun from under the pillow as the paper blind was kicked out by the blast of a shotgun. The mattress erupted into feathers and singed cloth as the buckshot charge slammed into the spot he had been but a moment earlier.

'Missed, you idiot!' someone snarled on the narrow veranda outside and Keel, crouched on the other side of the smouldering bedclothes, recognized the voice of Bruno Penn.

44

Then the torn blind was blown off its rollers by the second barrel of the shotgun. Keel rolled away, came up to his knees, glimpsed the silhouettes of two men out there as he brought up his six-gun and triggered three fast shots. Glass shattered, wood splintered and one of the dark shapes slammed back, yelled briefly, and then disappeared over the flimsy rail. The second man cursed and started to run.

Keel lunged for the smashed window, leaned out his upper body and withdrew smartly as a six-gun roared and wood slivers tore past his face. He looked out again as he saw Bruno Penn skidding around the corner. He fired and Penn faltered, stumbled and fell sprawling.

Keel ran along the veranda and kicked the man's six-gun out of his reach as Penn tried to get to it. The wounded man grimaced up at the towering Keel.

'Got more lives . . . than a cat! You

45

. . . lost me my . . . job, damn you . . . '

Penn suddenly heaved forward, a knife glinting in his hand as he lunged upwards at Keel's belly. The rancher shot him through the head as feet pounded up the outside stairway and he spun, trying to remember how many shots he had fired.

It was Sheriff Andy Cole and some townsmen. Keel spoke quietly. 'Nothing for you to worry about here, Sheriff. Two men tried to kill me while I was in bed. Self-defence.'

'I'll decide that!' Cole snapped. 'After I've investigated!' He swung up the Colt pistol he held, cocking the hammer. 'Hand over your gun, Keel, you're goin' in the cells till I get the straight of this!'

Keel sighed and handed over his still smoking Colt. He might have known Cole wouldn't give him any kind of a break. There had been hostility between them since the day Keel had arrived in Anchor Basin.

But he didn't figure even Cole could

pin a murder charge on him over this fracas.

★ ★ ★

Keel spent a restless night in the cellblock of the San Antonio law office and when he heard low voices and boots coming down the flagged passage outside he got up off the bunk and went to the bars, expecting breakfast.

Instead, he was surprised to see Sheriff Cole leading McMann and Joel Askins towards him. Keel stepped back from the bars and waited.

'Mr McMann ain't bringin' any charges agin you, Keel, so that makes you lucky.'

As the sheriff fumbled at the door lock, Keel set his gaze on McMann. 'Why would he bring charges?' he asked.

'They were my men,' McMann said easily. 'And I look after people who work for me.'

'How about those you kick out?' Keel

watched the man's face straighten out and he smiled crookedly. 'Bruno said I lost him his job with you . . . I guess that's why he and the other one I threw down the saloon stairs tried to nail me.'

'I dismissed them, yes, but they had worked for me for some time and I don't forget my people. You're right, though: it must've been pure vindictiveness on their part and I believe Sheriff Cole is satisfied with that explanation.'

Cole nodded quickly. 'Whatever you say, Mr McMann. I'm here to oblige whenever I can . . . ' He held the door open and Keel took his hat off the end of the bunk, jammed it on and stepped out into the passage.

He picked up his gun and belongings in the front office. 'You get out of town quick as you like,' Cole told him.

'Aim to. I'll be driving that Hereford all day to reach my spread.'

As he started for the door, McMann said, 'Adam, we somehow ended up at loggerheads last night and I'm willing to admit that perhaps I went about things the wrong way — I'd still like you to guide me into the Warbonnets.' He lifted a hand quickly as Keel started to speak, shaking his head. 'Just guide me into the general area where I might encounter the mountain cat — I have men who can flush him out. Money doesn't seem to mean much to you, even though I understand you need some at this juncture, so perhaps this will appeal to you: you're an outdoors man and I've learned you are very handy with firearms . . . suppose you and I have a competition?'

He paused but Keel waited silently.

'I'll lend you the Sharps-Borchadt rifle and I'll use my Remington. If I win, you guide me to the Warbonnets; if — I say *if* — I lose, I'll buy you a second seed bull for your breeding project. That sporting enough for you?'

Keel held the man's gaze, seeing the expectancy on McMann's face — the expectation that Keel would not, could not, refuse such a challenge.

But Keel shook his head. 'Not

interested, McMann. I have enough work to keep me busy all summer.'

McMann forced a smile. 'You sound as if you would expect to lose!'

Keel shrugged. 'I might lose: I might win . . . either way I'm just not interested. The sooner you realize that, McMann, the better. There's an Indian, a Mescalero, who knows those hills as good as I do — '

McMann's face clouded. 'I don't deal with Indians!'

Keel nodded gently as if he should have expected that. 'Well, can't help you . . . *Adios.*'

He nodded to Askins who seemed uncertain about what he should do here, and then went out into the street, hurrying towards the livery. He wanted to get on the trail with his bull before the full heat of the day.

Standing in the doorway of the law office, McMann slammed his gold-headed gun cane against the doorframe. His well-fed face was ugly as he gritted, 'That's the last time that man walks away from me!' He swung his hot gaze to Askins. 'You understand, Joel? *The very last time!*'

Askins looked uncomfortable as he nodded. 'I savvy, boss.'

* * *

Keel didn't believe it.

He had been driving the fairly co-operative bull for over two hours and San Antone had been lost in the dust and behind a ridge by now. The trail was lonely, rarely travelled by anyone, except Keel and old Stew Ormond.

And yet there was someone standing beside it up ahead. The glare fooled him at first into thinking it was some drifter waiting for a stage that would never come along this trail. But then he tugged his hat down lower to shade his eyes and he got a good look at the person up ahead.

Damned if it wasn't Della Lorrance! Complete with carpetbag.

4

Stubborn!

Old Stew Ormond groped his way out of the barn, swearing for the millionth time at the opaque lenses growing across his eyes and sending him slowly blind. He knew they were called cataracts and there was an operation that was sometimes successful in restoring clear vision — for a time at least — but the knowledge did him no good.

It would cost too much to send him to the East Coast cities to have the operation and he had no intention of allowing Adam Keel to pay for it. The man had enough to worry about just keeping the ranch going, and now that he had finally taken the plunge and bought himself a seed bull, well, expenses could only increase.

Anyway, Adam had done enough for him over the years, not the least giving him a home here on the Anchor for the rest of his life if he wanted it that way. Well, old Stew was mighty grateful, but he knew when he was totally blind he would rise early one morning and find his way to the rim of Anchor Canyon — only a couple of miles and he knew he could do it because he had been practising, walking there with his eyes tight-shut — then, well, he would relieve Adam of any further responsibility. It was only fair.

At the door of the barn, he felt the warmth of the sun on his grizzled face, rubbed a hand over his bristly silver whiskers and squinted. There was mostly glare but he could make out a few things, shadowy and indistinct. But having lived here so long with Keel he knew what the grey blobs were: the cottonwood tree and the forge beneath it; that old Conestoga wagon with the busted wheel Adam had bought for no good reason that either of them could see, except it made a good nesting place for the chickens; then, there was the long shape that was the water trough and pump this side of the corrals.

He stopped recounting and cocked his head, listening. His hearing wasn't the best but it had grown more acute since his sight had started to fade, and he heard the sound of horses. Or could it be one horse and the seed bull . . . ?

Stew Ormond's old heart increased its rate of pumping. 'That you, Adam?' he called in his cracked voice, holding to the edge of the barn door. When there was no answer he called again, louder.

'He'll be along shortly, old-timer.' The voice made him jump it was so close and he flinched and tried to pull away as a hand grabbed his arm. The grip tightened and the voice spoke again, this time with a little amusement in it. 'Now where you goin', Pop? Way your eyes are you could do yourself an injury, wanderin' around by yourself.

Here, lemme help you to the house porch.'

Stew, heart really hammering now, pulled back, dug in his worn boot heels. 'I don't wanna go up to the house! Who you, anyways? I dunno you . . . '

'You're right there, Pop — but my name's Curly Sampson and this here's my pard, Shorty Fischer. Say 'howdy' to ol' Stew, Shorty.'

'Howdy,' said a gruff voice and from its position Stew knew the man was mounted. Then saddle leather creaked as Fischer dismounted and he felt the man take his other arm. 'Pop, you're goin' to the house whether you like it or not.'

Ormond struggled but was no match for the hard strength of the two men as they dragged him towards the cabin.

'Leave me be, dammit!' he croaked, panting now with his futile efforts. 'What you fellers want? You best not be here when Adam comes.'

Curly laughed. 'Hell, no, Pop, we'll be long gone — but you'll still be here.'

They were at the foot of the three steps that led up to the porch now and he writhed and wrenched as they lifted his feet clear of the ground with no effort at all and deposited him on the porch.

'What the *hell* d'you want? Ain't no money here!'

'Mebbe not,' Shorty said curtly, pushing Ormond through the door now into the cabin. 'But there's money to be made here just the same, right, Curly?'

'Couldn't be righter, Shorty, ol' pard. Say, Pop, you left the oil lamp burnin'. Ain't only wasteful, it's downright dangerous. I mean, if you was to stumble agin the table — like *this*! — why, the lamp could fall just like it did and burst, an' the flame could set the oil afire. By God, Shorty, it's happenin' just like I said!'

'Yeah — poor ol' feller's too dang blind to be left alone in safety. Why, lookit them flames now licking at the dry table wood *and* the floor-boards . . .'

'Hell! The burnin' oil's reached the far wall over there. Hey, we best get outa here. C'mon, Pop . . . aw will you look at that? He fell . . . hit his head on that chair, din' he . . . ?'

'I dunno,' Shorty said, as he picked up the chair and broke it across the shouting oldster's head. 'Yeah, guess you're right. He did hit his head on the chair . . . '

The flames were roaring now and there was no chance of saving the cabin. Shorty Fischer and Curly Sampson got out, leaving the unconscious old man sprawled in the middle of the floor, the cabin burning down around him.

They were tempted to tear down the corrals and let out the horses, but they wanted it to look like an accident, so with regret, they rode away from Adam Keel's Anchor spread slowly, stopping on the low hogback under a tree to sit saddle and roll smokes as they watched the cabin burn to the ground.

'The hell're you doing way out here on foot?'

Keel hadn't aimed to ask quite like that, but as he rode his horse up to where Della Lorrance stood beside her carpetbag, it just burst out of him.

The Hereford, freed from his hazing — Keel hadn't used a nose-rope so soon after Doc Dellasandro's surgery — wandered off into the shade searching for some juicy grass.

The girl's face showed its bruises this morning as she looked up at him, eyes dull, mouth unsmiling. 'I thought I'd walk out to your ranch but I — well, I haven't done a lot of walking lately . . . and this heat . . . '

He didn't dismount, hooked a boot heel on the horn and took out cigarette papers and tobacco, starting to build a smoke.

'What makes you think you'd be welcome at my ranch?'

I . . . thought you might . . . change

58

your mind about me. Shell kicked me out last night . . . he won't take me back.' She wiped the back of a hand across her mouth. 'Have you any water?'

He finished rolling his cigarette, placed it between his lips and fired up before reaching for the saddle canteen and handing it to her. She took it quickly, uncorked it and took a long pull, then splashed some into her dust-streaked face. She handed it back with a quiet 'Thank you.'

Keel hooked it back on the saddle, looking at her thoughtfully as he smoked. 'Don't McMann *ever* give up?'

Her eyes blazed. 'Do you think he *sent* me here, for God's sake? Oh, you're unbelievable, Adam Keel! D'you think I'd voluntarily walk all this way in the heat just to wait for you so I could . . . seduce you or whatever you think I might have in mind, just because Shell McMann wants you to help him find some damn cat?'

'Crossed my mind.'

She didn't quite stamp her foot but came mighty close. She placed her hands on her slim hips. 'I wish I had a gun! I'd shoot you! You insulted me last night and now you've done it again! Oh, to hell with you! I should've had more sense than to think that you — you'd show any compassion for my situation.'

She picked up her heavy carpetbag and staggered a little as she started around his horse. He didn't move, kept smoking. He didn't turn to watch as she struggled back along the trail, the carpetbag dragging in the dust now. She panted loudly, obviously so he would hear.

'I didn't cut your sign anywheres between here and San Antone,' he said, still without looking round. 'But I did notice a few hoofprints . . . ' He hipped suddenly, surprised to see how far she had walked already. 'Couldn't be that someone rode you out here and left you to wait for me, could it?'

She didn't answer, although he

thought she hesitated a little and then she dropped the bag suddenly, screamed as she picked up a rock and hurled it at the bull as it stood facing her, coming out of the shade now.

'Get this animal away from me!' she cried, but Keel was amused. Then her next missile struck the bull on his tender nose and he snorted and bellowed, forequarters swaying as pain surged through him.

Then he wheeled and ran back into the trees, still bellowing, crashing through the underbrush, maddened by the pain. Keel swore, tossed the cigarette into the dust of the trail and settled in saddle, ramming home the spurs. The girl ran towards him and he wrenched the reins so hard the horse almost fell.

'Don't leave me alone out here!' she cried. 'I-I've had enough of this isolation! Let me ride double. Please!'

'Get outa the way!' Keel snapped, as she grabbed the stirrup and held on, pleading with him now. But she stayed put, almost falling as she followed the manoeuvrings of the mount. Keel swore, reached down, twisted fingers in her chestnut hair and flung her back to sprawl in the dust. 'Sorry, didn't mean that. But the damn bull's getting away!'

'You filthy son of a bitch! That's the first time anyone's ever preferred a bull to *me*!'

He laughed, couldn't help himself, then spurred after the Hereford now lumbering well ahead and starting up the slope of a ridge, still bellowing occasionally.

The girl remained seated in the dust, almost in tears, as Keel spurred through the trees, losing time as he sat higher in the saddle than the bull and had to weave and dodge around low-hanging branches.

By the time he cleared the trees, the bull was almost at the top of the ridge and when the big animal reached the crest it turned, snorting, and he saw the reddish vapour around its head and knew the rock had burst Doc Dellasandro's sutures.

He started the horse up the slope — then suddenly hauled rein, standing in the stirrups.

The bull staggered sideways, paused briefly, then fell over on to its side, raising a cloud of dust.

Keel thought he heard a very distant sound — like a hammer striking a board at the far end of a canyon, just a faint echo lingering briefly.

Face grim, he spurred his mount on up the slope.

⋆   ⋆   ⋆

Sheriff Andy Cole was packing his pipe in the doorway of the law office, beefy shoulder leaning against the frame, when he saw the dust cloud of a fast-approaching rider coming in from the south-west. He paused with his thumb pressing down the tobacco into the cherrywood bowl, squinting.

'Judas priest! That looks like . . .

Goddamn, it is! It's Keel and he's got the bit between his teeth!'

He dropped the pipe into his pocket and swung back into his office, reaching for his gunrig slung on the wall pegs and his hat . . . but he knew he was going to be too late.

Keel would reach McMann's Pullman on the sidetrack long before he could get there and head off the trouble he knew was about to explode in the rich man's face . . .

⋆   ⋆   ⋆

The lawman wasn't the only one to observe Keel's thundering approach. As he skidded his lathered mount to a halt near the Pullman, and hit the ground running, two men stepped out from the shade at one end of the car.

'Hold up there, mister!' called Curly Sampson. 'You can't go in there.'

Keel glanced at the hardcases, hands held over their gunbutts. He turned back towards the Pullman and kept striding. Sampson swore and Shorty Fischer ran at Keel, six-gun coming out of leather. Adam Keel turned sharply, his own gun in hand, and whipped the startled Shorty to his knees.

Sampson propped momentarily, cursed, then ran forward, bringing up his own gun. Keel shot a leg out from under him and when the man went down howling, he kicked his gun out of reach and planted a boot under the man's jaw. Then he frowned, leaned down and sniffed. Face harder than ever, he leaned over Shorty and sniffed, too.

'Reckon that's about far enough, Adam.'

Keel straightened slowly, seeing Joel Askins standing at the foot of the steps with drawn and cocked six gun. McMann stood at the top of the steps, looking a mite uneasy. There was movement behind him in the dimness and Keel's mouth tightened as he caught a glimpse of chestnut hair.

'The woman got back here fast enough — she have a horse hidden out there by the trail?'

Askins shrugged. 'Drop the gun, Adam.'

Keel hesitated, put the Colt back into its holster, reckless defiance in his eyes. Askins' jaw hardened but he nodded briefly, accepting the move for now: after all, he was the one holding the cocked gun.

'What's your hurry, Adam?' asked McMann.

'I want to see your Remington or the Sharps.'

'Oh? I thought you'd had a good look at them last night, or — No! You've changed your mind and want to accept my challenge of a target-shoot, have you?'

The look on Keel's face made McMann wince involuntarily. 'I want to see if either one's been fired recently. Someone just shot my seed bull. From about a mile away, I'd reckon . . . '

'Good heavens! Who would do such a

thing . . . ?' Then McMann arched his eyebrows. 'Are you accusing *me*?'

'You're the one who likes the long shots.'

McMann spread his hands. 'But I haven't left town all morning! Ask Joel — or better still, ask the sheriff. He was here trying to find out if I was really going to put in those spur tracks or scrap the plans if you didn't agree to guide me into the Warbonnets. Of course, I told him that was all past history now, that you'd made your decision, and I would make mine in due course.'

'You're a liar,' Keel said flatly and McMann's breath hissed in between his teeth.

'Joel!' he snapped, and Askins stepped forward, swinging his gun at Keel's head.

Keel ducked under and came up close to Askins, looking into the angry eyes, and coldly brought up his knee between the man's legs. Askins groaned and swayed and started to fall. Keel twisted the gun from his hand and swung towards the steps. McMann had turned swiftly back into the car and Keel leapt up the steps, shouldered aside Della Lorrance as she tried to block the doorway, saw McMann scrabbling for his gun stick where it lay across a chair.

Keel hit him across the back of the head with the six-gun barrel and McMann grunted, floundered to his knees. Keel snatched up the gun stick placed it at an angle to the floor and brought his boot down across it. The wood splintered and the long thin barrel twisted almost U-shaped.

'Oh, you damn *fool!*' cried the girl. 'He'll kill you now!'

Keel gave her a scathing look, grabbed the nickel-plated Remington from the wall and swung it by the barrel against the door frame. The stock splintered and he smashed it again, damaging the doorway but also denting the action. He flung the remains out into the yard and was bringing down the Sharps-Borchadt when the sheriff's breathless voice snapped, 'Hold it right there, Keel! *Right* there! Or I swear I'll blow your spine in two!'

5

Big Trouble

'You're in big trouble this time, Adam!

McMann was holding a cold cloth against the swelling on the back of his head, his curled black hair dishevelled. The girl stood by with a basin of cold water and fresh folded rags draped around the edge. She changed the cloths whenever McMann signalled.

Sheriff Cole had the cuffs on Keel who sat slumped in an overstuffed chair near the cold fireplace in the Pullman's parlour. It was a little crowded, what with the lawman and a pale-faced Joel Askins squeezing in as well as the others.

'You just say the word, Mr McMann, and I'll lock him up and throw away the key.' Cole's eyes blazed at Keel. 'Been waitin' a long time to get you like this,

Keel. You went too blame far.'

'Yes, he did,' McMann said coldly, an iciness in his eyes that made Keel just a mite uneasy. 'Wounding one of my men, attacking others — not to mention me. Then destroying valuable property.' He shook his head gently, winced, snatched a fresh cloth from the girl and held it against his throbbing wound. 'I can be a forgiving man, Keel, but not this — that Remington was my favourite gun and it cost thousands.'

'That Hereford bull only cost me a coupla hundred, but it was just as valuable to me as your gun was to you,' Keel told him.

McMann spread his hands. 'And you unhesitatingly accused me of shooting the animal! You overestimate your importance to me, Keel. You were a potential employee but you refused my very fair offers — I'm afraid I lost interest in you after you killed those two men last night.'

'That's the difference between us,

McMann — I haven't lost interest in
you.'

McMann paled a little, swivelled his
gaze to the sheriff. 'I believe there was
some sort of veiled threat there,
Sheriff.'

Cole nudged Keel's legs roughly with
his boot. 'You watch your mouth! Mr
McMann was with me all mornin'. He
couldn't've shot your damn bull.'

Keel lifted his gaze to Joel Askins.
'You were always a pretty good rifle
shot, Joel.'

Askins snorted. 'You're crazy! Even
crazier than when you rode in the
Border Patrol.'

'Well, I'll tell you just how crazy I
am.' Keel's bleak eyes roved over
everyone present. 'This *whore* played
her part well, delayed me along the
trail, managed to run off my bull so
whoever was waiting could get a shot at
it *and* to give Sampson and Fischer
time to get out to my place.'

Della Lorrance blinked, her jaw
dropping slightly, and Keel frowned:

her surprise seemed almost genuine.

'I know nothing about Sampson and Fischer,' she said but fell silent at a glare from McMann.

'Why would those two want to go out to your place, Keel?' he asked calmly enough.

'After I reached my bull and saw the bullet-hole in him, I was ready to come back here and tear your throat out, but I saw a smudge of smoke in the hills — right about where my place is . . . When I reached it, I found the cabin had burned to the ground. Old Stew Ormond — or what was left of him — was sprawled on the floor near an overturned table. There was glass from the oil lamp on the floor. Looked like he'd stumbled over a chair or something, overturned the table and the lamp broke and set fire to the cabin.'

'Well, that sounds a reasonable explanation,' McMann said. 'I believe you mentioned the old man was nearly blind; accidents like that happen all the time.'

Keel watched the rich man steadily.

'Not to old Stew. He knew every inch of that cabin, knew where every piece of furniture was. He may've forgotten to blow out the lamp, but he wouldn't trip over anything.'

There was silence for a few moments. The girl looked actually distressed now and her eyes were large.

'What — what're you saying?' she asked quietly, and McMann frowned at her, looking annoyed.

'Reckon I'm saying someone set it up to make it look like an accident.'

'You crazy bastard!' snapped Cole. 'You always was an edgy sonuver, figuring folk were doin' stuff just to rile you. Hell, you keep to yourself so much folk don' know what to make of you!'

'Which is maybe *why* they try to rile me now and again,' Keel replied. 'See what I'll do.'

Cole snorted. 'Hell, we *know* what you'll do! You get red-headed about it and start pushin' in a few faces. I dunno how many times I've warned you . . . '

'We're getting off the subject!' snapped McMann. 'Keel, are you seriously suggesting that two of my men attacked your old companion and then deliberately burned down your ranch house — with him inside?'

'I am. Tell you why: both Sampson and Fischer stink of woodsmoke. I smelt it on their clothes outside.'

McMann made an exasperated sound and motion. 'Good God, man! That's probably only camp-fire smoke!'

Keel gestured to the Pullman. 'Why would they light camp-fires when they've got the dining-room next door? You told me you feed your men well, McMann, that they might not eat at the same table as you, but they get the best of grub and — to quote you — 'they eat in rich surroundings'.'

McMann sighed. 'They were off-duty today. I don't know where they went or what they did. They were free to fill in the day however they wished. They could have made coffee beside the trail or — '

'Forget it, McMann. You're flogging a dead horse. You sent them to burn my spread . . . maybe leaving Stew there was their own idea, I'll concede that.'

McMann shook his head slowly. 'Sheriff, what *is* this man talking about?'

'I dunno, sir. He's a troublemaker from way back. You bring whatever charges you want and I'll see he's locked away for a long time.'

McMann frowned, swung his head slowly towards Keel. 'Well, the future doesn't look too bright for you, Keel I'm sorry it's come to this, but you leave me little choice. You've gone much too far. But, I can be a reasonable man, and if you genuinely believe — mistakenly, I hasten to add — that what you claim happened was my fault, well, I suppose I can understand your reactions, you being the kind of man you are.' He smiled slowly. 'However, my men are paid well to take risks and I'm sure we could come to some kind of arrangement so you don't spend too much time — or even any — in jail.'

Cole was astonished. 'Now, wait up, Mr McMann! There's been a crime committed here and . . . '

He let his words fade away under McMann's cold stare and the rich man brought back his smile for Keel. 'The Warbonnets are still there, I believe, Adam . . . '

Della made a gasping sound but quickly left the room, murmuring that she would get some fresh water as McMann flung her a savage look. Keel remained impassive.

'I wouldn't work for you, McMann, if you offered me ten thousand bucks.'

McMann sighed, spread his hands.

'Well, Sheriff, I've done all I can to smooth this out — and it seems I've failed. So, charges will be brought against you, Keel, and I'll make them as severe as the law allows. Sheriff Cole, I'll give you a statement and my attorney will be with you in a few days. I'm sure I don't need to stay around for the trial . . . ?'

'Sure not, Mr McMann, a busy man like you. No, I'll lock Keel up in my cells and we'll hold the trial as soon as your man gets here.'

McMann smiled his pleasure. 'I'm sure you'll see that the most severe penalty allowed by law is invoked, Sheriff . . . ' He paused to make sure Cole understood and the lawman nodded emphatically, hauled Keel to his feet.

'You leave it to me, Mr McMann. This feller's up on attempted murder as well as destruction of your property. I know, he ain't got any money to pay you back, but he can work it out on the county chain-gang. Then there's the assault charges an' I still ain't happy about those men he killed last night.'

McMann smiled again, looking at the prisoner now. 'What a mess you've made of things, Keel! And to think you could still have your ranch — *and* your friend — and your bull. Plus five hundred dollars to boot. Oh, well, I hope we've all learned a lesson from this. Goodbye, Adam. It's not likely we'll ever meet again.'

'Don't bet on it.'

McMann's smile vanished at the chilling implication of Keel's words and Cole curled a lip and shoved the rancher roughly towards the door.

'Come on!'

As he went down the steps, Keel glimpsed Della Lorrance's pale face at one of the windows.

★   ★   ★

In the cellblock, Sheriff Cole shoved Keel roughly down the passage and when they reached the first cell with its open door, he swung the prisoner around suddenly and drove a fist into his midriff.

Keel gagged, grunted, and dropped to his knees. Cole twisted fingers in his shirt collar and flung him violently into the cell to sprawl across the flagstones of the floor. Cole came in, heaved the man onto the bunk and backhanded him brutally, as he sat on the edge, trying to gather his senses.

'Been waitin' a long time for this, Keel!' Cole told him as he hit him again.

'Had to — wait till you — got the cuffs on me — to do it,' Keel gritted.

Cole sneered and punched him in the face. 'You tripped comin' in, hit your face on the edge of the bunk. That's what give you the bloody nose — and the split lip. Oh — your lip *ain't* split?' He swung another punch and laughed. 'Well, it is now!'

Then Keel came up off the bunk and drove the top of his head under the sheriff's jaw, knocking the man across the cell, Cole's arms flailing for balance. The lawman roared and started for his gun and Keel hit him in the face with his manacles. Cole went down, blood spraying across the flag-stones.

Keel knelt swiftly and rolled the man over so he could get his six-gun. Then boots pounded down the passage and

Cole's deputy, Arnie Grissom, came surging in, flinging Keel back by the hair, driving a kick into his ribs. He grabbed the semi-conscious Cole, dragged him out of the cell and slammed the door shut, turning the keys that were dangling in the lock. He was a big man, normally slow-moving and with a perpetually vague look. He glared at Keel.

'You can stay cuffed just for that, Adam!'

Keel said nothing, watched Arnie get the groggy sheriff on his feet and lead him away down the passage. Somehow he figured he hadn't seen the last of the lawman.

★   ★   ★

There was a tin dish of stale-looking water on an upended box in a corner of the cell and Keel scooped up a couple of handfuls, splashing his bloody face. He wiped it as well as he could on part of the coarse bunk blanket and sat

81

down on the bed, looking at the manacles on his wrists.

Cole had put them on as tightly as he could: the flesh was already swollen and he was losing feeling in his hands. He smiled crookedly. That was typical of Andy Cole.

The man never forgot a grudge. The one he held against Keel was only partly real.

It had happened five years ago when Keel had first come here and bought Anchor Basin and set up his ranch. Seems that Cole and his weak brother, Tully, had had their eye on the land and were trying to raise the money to buy it when Keel came in with a cash-on-the-barrelhead offer. As the original owner wanted money badly to go to Boston to see his ailing daughter, he had taken Keel's offer at once and quit town.

Cole had just been made sheriff and he tried to intimidate Keel into quitting before he had even started. They fought and Cole learned quickly that Keel was a mighty stubborn man — and likely the toughest *hombre* ever to come to this neck of the woods.

Meantime, Tully had gotten drunk again, gambled away the money that they'd managed to get together and ended up a full-blown drunk. Andy always blamed Keel for his brother's drinking, claimed Keel's actions drove Tully to it. The hostility between them hadn't lessened in the ensuing five years; if anything, it had increased.

He glanced up now as the sheriff appeared, holding a wet cloth against his bruised mouth. He called Keel to the bars and the prisoner obeyed warily, but Andy simply removed the cuffs. Keel winced as blood flowed back into his aching fingers, rubbed them briskly. Cole managed a bloody smirk.

'If you think I'm goin' soft, just forget it. I can afford to treat you right for a spell — know why? 'Cause I know you're headin' for the chain-gang and the gang-boss happens to be an old friend of yours.' He paused, unable to stifle a short, hard laugh. 'Remember

Tully? 'Course you do. Well, he's a reformed drunk now an' they're the ones work hardest to show everyone just how good they really are. Prison governor has give him a free hand to keep that gang runnin' smooth an' he ain't had one successful escape yet! Yeah, you're headed for hard time, Keel, but you'll never do your *full* time. I can guarantee that!'

Still laughing, he walked away, almost swaggering.

★　★　★

The very comfortable Pullman swayed very little as the special train ordered by McMann drew it along the rails, heading north-east out of San Antonio.

McMann and Della sat opposite each other at the dinner-table, the lamps burning in their silver gimbals, the chef's assistant coming in to clear away the dinner dishes. McMann lowered his wine glass and snapped at the man to leave it, to come back later. The man hurried out and Della looked at McMann through the smoke from her scented cigarette which she held in a long, carved ivory holder he had bought her in Cairo.

'I thought you'd be in a happier mood, Shell, now that you've had your little victory over Adam Keel.'

He lowered his glass slowly, his eyes steady on her face. '*Little* victory, Della? I consider it more than that. The man insulted me, assaulted me, killed two of my men and wounded another . . . now he'll be going to jail for several years. I believe that's much more than a small victory.'

Although she didn't show it, Della felt tense inside, Andre's wonderful food heaving a little in her stomach. She shouldn't have opened her mouth: she had misjudged McMann's mood. He had had his triumph, all right, but somehow it hadn't satisfied him and she knew he wouldn't rest until he had done something more — something that only his twisted mind would consider as totally satisfactory.

Which boded mighty ill for Adam Keel, of course.

'Well, you certainly taught Keel a lesson, Shell,' she said, smiling, heart hammering, choosing her words very carefully, as he continued to give her that unwavering stare. 'The man was a fool to think he could defy you.'

'Ye-es . . . but for a time there, I began to think that you held a little — sympathy — for him.'

'Whatever gave you that idea, Shell?' she asked, smiling charmingly. 'The one thing that did surprise me was Sampson and Fischer killing that old man . . . '

He said nothing, his face impassive. Della shrugged, awkwardly.

'I did think — they'd gone too far there.'

'That Remington's going to cost a small fortune to have put right,' McMann said obtusely. 'Perhaps I'll have another built, this time with one of those German scope-sights I've been reading about . . . I'll amuse myself by testing it on some really big game this time. I don't need Keel and I'm no longer interested in that mountain cat.'

She arched her eyebrows and before she could stop herself, said, 'But you did offer to drop charges against him if he'd change his mind.' She let it hang and was surprised when he suddenly smiled.

'You haven't learned a lot about me even after all our years together, have you, Della? It's not what you are, but how you are perceived. Now Sheriff Cole witnessed that offer I made Keel. He'll tell people that I'm a very reasonable man, not vindictive, bent over backwards to give Keel a break. You see? Image, Della, image. You, of all people, ought to understand that. You wear the best clothes, latest fashions from Paris and Rome on occasion, you move in the very best social circles on my arm and you are perceived as a sophisticate, a rich man's companion.' The smile tightened as he added, 'But we all know that underneath every-thing, you are still no more than a whore, paid for her services.'

Della stiffened, blood draining from her face. When she spoke her words were barely audible.

'I know what *I* am, Shell.'

He laughed, throwing back his head. 'Careful, my dear! There may be quicksand where you are about to tread — and I must remind you that whores are only a dime-a-dozen to men like me.' The smile faded completely. 'You understand?'

She could do nothing but nod meekly, trying to breathe, feeling as if she was choking. She had been utterly stupid to even skirt the edges of censure with this man.

She somehow forced a smile and raised her wine glass. 'Well, you got even with Keel, Shell, that's the main thing. Let's drink to that. You should be a happy man now.'

She sipped but he didn't touch his glass. 'Not as happy, as you may think

— Keel is the only man who has so insulted me, *and* laid a hand on me and still lived. I do not like living with that knowledge. So I may toy with him for a while, see that he has a truly hard time in prison. I want to see the man *broken* before eventually . . . '

He shrugged, letting it hang.

She was bone-white now as she watched him pierce a cigar with a gold doo-dad and ring the little silver table bell for Andre's assistant to light the smoke for him.

Well, she shouldn't be surprised that he would feel like this: she'd always suspected he was more than a little mad.

6

Chain Gang

Judge Luther Michaels sentenced Adam Keel to five years on the county chain-gang *'or such other place of incarceration it seems prudent to move you to during your period of detention'*.

'The sentence would be much harsher except the charge of murdering Bruno Penn and the man known only as Mooney has not been proved to my satisfaction. In my opinion it was a clear case of self-defence.' The judge banged the gavel once, loudly, in the hushed courtroom. 'Case closed.'

There was a lot of murmuring in the crowd and someone gave a half-hearted cheer but quickly subsided into silence at a scowl from the judge. Michaels stood, glowered around at the dispersing crowd but avoided looking directly at Keel who was being ushered through the side door by Sheriff Andy Cole.

'Don't wanna keep Tully waitin', do we, Keel?' Cole chuckled. 'He come himself specially to collect you.'

Keel grunted: he had expected nothing less.

The pick-up wagon waited outside in the hot, bright sunlight, big Tully Cole perched up on the driving seat. A scar-faced guard with the lobe missing off his left ear, stood chewing tobacco beside the rear door. Instead of a canopy on the wagon, the back was built in with interlaced iron strapping, a heavy brass padlock and bolt on the single door.

There were already four dishevelled and miserable prisoners chained to the floor as the sheriff shoved Keel roughly into the arms of the guard.

'All yours, Burl.'

'Damn right.' The guard shoved Keel away hard and slammed him against the side of the cage as he swung open the door and took his arm and pushed him up the short steps. In his ankle chains and manacles, Keel stumbled and Burl Becker hit him with his billy across the kidneys. 'We got five years together, Keel, you an' me. Be best you learn what I like and don't like right off — so no more stumblin' about, OK?'

As he deftly bolted Keel's chains to the rings in the heavy floor, Tully Cole flicked a salute to his brother, leaned back and spat on Keel through the bars.

'Been waitin' a long time for this moment, Keel. Just a reminder — you ain't your own man any more, mister. Now you're mine and we get you out to the compound and you'll do every leetle thing I say — or you'll find out what happens to prisoners who don't jump when I say so!'

'Nice to see you again, Tully,' Keel gritted but Burl Becker punched him in the mouth.

'You speak only when you got permission to, Keel! You'd best remember that.'

Tully chuckled. 'Too bad you ain't

comin' along to see how we'll be bringin' Keel down to the common denominator, Andy.'

'Yeah, I'd sure like to see it. Mebbe I'll come visit once in a while, see how he's gettin' along.'

'Any time, Brother, any time. All right, Burl, let 'er roll.'

The guard, now in the driving seat, cracked the whip over the six-horse team and they leaned into the collars and slowly the heavy wagon crunched out across the plaza with its load of human misery.

San Antone folk had lined-up to jeer and wave off the prisoners, especially Adam Keel.

'Thanks for losin' this town a hundred jobs and a freight line, Keel, you son of a bitch!'

'They shoulda shot *you*, not the damn bull!'

'If you live through the next five years, don't bother comin' back — we don't want you here, Keel!'

More jeers followed the creaking

wagon out of town and the quarter-breed prisoner chained next to Keel bared chipped yellow teeth and said, 'See you got a lotta friends in this town.'

'Yeah, best one of all is the warden.' Keel flicked his eyes upwards to Tully Cole's broad back.

The 'breed sobered quickly. 'Jesus! Man, I ain't gonna hang around with you! That Tully's the meanest son of a bitch in the whole South-west.'

Keel shook his head. 'Wrong — *I* am. They just dunno it yet.'

★ ★ ★

The prisoners were housed in long, draughty sheds that leaked when it rained, were ice-boxes when the cold winds blew, and were stifling at night with every shutter and door bolted on the outside.

There were a few trusted prisoners who had bunks to sleep in but the vast majority had only a common long wooden bench without benefit of mattress or bedclothes. A long chain ran through ringbolts and over the leg irons' chains, fitted each night by one of the trusties who had a bunk and mattress to himself. No one ever got much sleep and the hard boards rubbed a man's skin off his bones. Some turned to callouses, some to suppurating sores. The only treatment was a dab of iodine by one of the trusties, if he wasn't too lazy to walk across to the sick bay and pick up a bottle and some cotton.

Food was minimal, mostly bread, sometimes containing grain, and a watery vegetable soup that occasionally held a chunk of meat. One day a week a halfway decent meal of beef and potatoes was served up to the men doing road work, not through compassion, but through practicality. Tully Cole, during his fight against alcoholism, had learned that a man needed protein for energy — and as he was being paid extra by a stageline to get the road through the wilderness finished by a certain date, he figured he could afford to feed his workers one decent meal a week.

The road was over some of the toughest country this side of the Badlands. It was to run through thick, tick-infested scrub that housed many snakes and brush rats whose urine carried a disease called *leptospirosis*. This was a chronic, debilitating illness that wasted a man away but which Tully Cole saw as no excuse for any prisoner not doing his allotted work.

Those who fell below the impractical schedule he had set tasted the lash, or the billies or cane rods of the guards. If they were stupid enough to retaliate, even raise a fist without striking, they were introduced to Tully's special place, *Hell's Kennel*. It was a four-foot cube made of corrugated iron, built out by itself, away from any vestige of shade. No man could stretch out or even draw up his knees comfortably. Certainly it was too low for most men to sit up and in the summer heat it grew hot enough to bake a cake.

Those who tasted what Tully called a *rest period* in the Kennel were never quite the same when they emerged. Most moved much more slowly, suffered excruciating joint pains, and some were vague, almost dim-witted after the ordeal.

Very few men were strong enough to emerge pretty much the same as when they had entered.

Keel was only on the gang for a month before he earned himself a rest period of three days, without food or water. His crime was picking up the 'wrong' shovel from a heap of seven. The guard — Burl Becker, as it happened — didn't like the handle and slammed Keel across the neck with his cane. 'You deef as well as dumb! The *big* one, damnit!'

Keel's head felt as if it was exploding as he staggered, dropped the tool. It landed across Becker's heavy boots and couldn't have hurt in any way, but the guard snarled, chose to believe it had been deliberate, and lashed Keel twice across the hunched shoulders with the cane. Keel snatched the rod from the man and Becker jumped back, hand on gun butt.

'Drop it! Or I'll shoot you down like a dog!'

Keel hesitated, the others around him ceasing work to watch, holding their breaths. The cane was raised and Becker's scarred face paled a little, not believing Keel could be so stupid as to openly attack him . . . but Keel merely opened his hand and let the rod fall.

Becker curled a lip. 'You just earned yourself three days in the Kennel, Keel!'

Another guard helped Becker drag Keel across and he was bundled inside with a heavy boot against the base of his spine. The iron door clanged shut and almost burst his ear drums. The guards smashed their billies against the walls and roof, running the hardwood along the corrugations. His head spun and his ears rang for hours afterward.

But it was nothing compared to the discomfort he was already feeling, trying to wriggle around, inch by inch, so as to ease his aching joints. It took him a while to realize there was no such position and he wondered if he would be a cripple when he was eventually released.

He resorted to the only relief he knew: sending his mind far away from the site of his predicament, thinking back through the years to another time and place that, briefly, allowed him to forget this piece of hell where he now was.

All the way back to that sod hut that had been his parents' embryo ranch at the edge of the Panhandle when the Apaches had come out of the dusk and slaughtered his mother and father and bigger brother, and his sister, in utter terror, had shot herself while he stood there with his five-year-old face crumbling in horror.

Then the smell of the Indian who

had swept him up and carried him off with the raiding party to the Apacheria somewhere deep in the Sierras to the south. Three years of living like an Indian, being trained even at that tender age in survival, the use and making of weapons, planning for his entry into warriorhood. The memories of his 'white' life were slowly fading when . . .

A tough scout named Stew Ormond led in a punitive troop of cavalry and suddenly there was blood and fire and noise and murder all around him. Ormond had somehow recognized him as a white boy beneath all the grime and sunburn, taken him home with him to his wife on their lonely ranch in the foothills of the Warbonnets.

The Ormonds had raised him, Stew contracting out as an army scout when times were lean on the ranch. One morning, Mrs Ormond wouldn't wake up and, still just a shaver of ten, Keel had run eleven miles into town to alert the doctor.

Of course, it was too late to save her and when Stew had returned Keel had sobbed that it was all his fault, that he had scared the horse he had tried to catch and if he had ridden he might have had the doctor out in time to save Mrs Ormond.

Stew assured him nothing could have saved her: she had died in her sleep. But he kept the boy at his side after that until one day in his early teens, Keel had decided to go trail-herding. The rest of his growing-up was done on the cattle trails and he gained a reputation as a fighter, a man who would not be pushed past a certain point that only he knew. He had a natural affinity for guns and killed his first man in a gunfight in Abilene, Kansas, when he was nineteen. But folk soon realized he wouldn't turn to the gun every time he had trouble. He would settle it with his fists, or a bottle broken over the head of the troublemaker when he figured the argument was not worth a man's life to settle it.

The town marshal offered him a job as a deputy when the herd he was with paid-off and Keel accepted. He went on to many other law-badge jobs after that and finally joined the Border Patrol.

Soon afterwards the word came through that Ormond was missing in Mexico, thought to have been killed by bandits in the wild Sierras near Durango . . .

* * *

The crash of the door opening in the Kennel brought him back to the present. He was all knotted-up when Becker dragged him out and flung him on the ground, wrinkling his nose.

'Christ, you *stink*!' He kicked Keel hard. 'Git on over to the ablutions block and clean-up. *Crawl*, you son of a bitch!'

Keel had little choice, but he managed to somehow fight to his feet halfway there when he heard Tully Cole's voice.

'Bring that man here, Burl.'

Tully was seated at a small table in the shade of an awning on the administration building. There was a terracotta jug with beads of moisture on the outside beside his hand. Becker and the guard with him, held Keel more or less upright.

'You're a mess, Adam,' Tully said affably enough. 'Andy told me to expect you to behave like a hard-case and he was right. You've brought all this on yourself and I hope you've learned a lesson.' He arched his eyebrows and Becker rammed the end of his billy into Keel's already aching ribs.

'Answer the warden!'

Keel nodded slowly. 'Yessir,' he slurred and Tully frowned.

'I could hardly make that out. Oh, of course, you must be parched.' Tully indicated the terracotta jug. 'Go ahead. Have a drink. I'm not as heartless as some folk would have you believe. Go on. Take a deep draught. We have to get you back in shape for the road work . . . '

He chuckled as Burl, at Tully's order, handed Keel the jug. He almost dropped it, but it sure felt mighty cool against his calloused palms. He threw caution to the winds and drank deeply.

It tasted wonderful, a mite saline but that was usual with ground water in this country, and so-oooo soothing to his parched throat and gullet . . .

'More?' asked Tully solicitously and when Keel shook his head, murmured his thanks, the warden said, 'Well, learn by your experience, Adam. Show some sense. Just do as you're told and you'll have no more trouble. All right, Burl, let him get cleaned-up now.'

Halfway across the compound, Keel was suddenly gripped with clenching pains in his belly. He gasped, stumbled, bent double, hugging himself.

'The hell's wrong with you?' demanded Becker, shaking him. 'Come *on*!'

'Got — to — use — the — latrine'!
Keel gritted.

He started at a stumbling, staggering run towards the ablutions block which also housed the latrines. Somewhere behind him he thought he heard Tully Cole laughing.

Then Becker came up alongside him and said, 'Guess the warden forgot to tell you that water was for washin' the saddle-sores on his personal mount — full of Epsom salts!'

By that time, Keel had already found that out for himself.

★   ★   ★

That was only the beginning.

From that moment on, Adam Keel couldn't do *anything* right, no matter how much he tried. He paid for it with beatings and other *rest periods* in the Kennel. Some do-gooders visited the chain-gang compound and afterwards the leg irons were removed at night. Well, the other prisoners had *their* leg irons taken off at night.

But not Keel: he wore his twenty-four hours a day.

Then several prisoners, either currying favour with the guards or having been ordered to, took to making life an even greater hell for him. They would knock his food tray out of his hand; spill more food on his ragged clothes and this brought the rats to him at night-time, chewing at the soiled cloth — and his flesh. He was covered with infected bites.

He was prodded and pushed, trying to get him to throw the first punch in a fight, but he was wise enough to walk away from all of them. Except the few that other prisoners started by hitting him . . . even so, he was the one who got the blame. And the punishment — cane-rod across the shoulders, a billy under the ribs, heavy guard boots stomping on the leg-iron chains, scraping the rings deep into his flesh.

It went on and on. Someone put a live rattler on his sleeping bench but the snake slithered away and eventually bit one of the trusties. The man had died foaming at the mouth. Trusties were hated even more than the road-gang guards and no one raised the alarm until it was too late.

Keel looked like a scarecrow, hair wild and tousled and fouled with muck placed there by guards or other prisoners. He was not allowed to wash as often as the others. His boots were coming apart, but repairs were refused. The manacles rubbed his ankles raw and it was agony to move. So they made him run everywhere, at the double, no matter how menial or small the chore: run or have his legs cut from under him with the long, rattan rods and then suffer a kicking by a bunch of guards.

Tully came to look at him once when they were dragging him out of the Kennel at the end of one of his *rest periods*. He scowled as Keel raised his eyes and the warden saw the defiance still there.

He leaned down close, trying to keep from gagging at Keel's smell. 'I *will* break you, Adam! I *will*!'

Keel managed to grate, 'Do — your — worst.'

And he spat on Tully's boots. The warden kicked him, cursing. 'Another three days in the Kennel!' he screamed.

When he came out, Keel heard that there had been three attempts at escape. All had failed. Two of the men had been brought back, torn apart by Tully's special hounds. The third came in with a bullet in the back of his head and several more in his broken body . . . No one had ever escaped from Three Creeks Prison camp.

But Keel would.

He figured it was time to leave before they turned him into a permanent cripple or killed him.

He was leaving this hell-hole, and if it had to be by way of a bullet in the back, then he would still class it as a victory.

But he wanted more than that, so he

devised a plan that would give him a *real* triumph over Tully and Andy Cole and not forgetting the bastard who had put him here: Shelby McMann.

Yeah. It was time to go.

7

Breakout

Joel Askins wondered why McMann had invited him into the parlour of the big ranch house outside of Denver at this time of night.

Usually, after supper, McMann wanted to see no one but the woman, Della. Truth was, Askins wouldn't mind 'seeing' her himself now and again, but while he was a brave enough man, he wasn't stupid. And only a fool would try to cuckold someone like McMann.

Askins' curiosity was sparked even further when his boss offered him a drink of his malt whisky.

'Sit down and relax, Joel. It's some time since we've had a talk.'

Askins sat and rolled a cigarette while McMann fired up one of his cigars. 'Good whisky, boss.'

McMann grunted: it had to be good or he wouldn't drink it. 'Joel, you once remarked that Keel was a crazy — *bastard* I believe was the word you used. Crazy like he used to be when you and he rode for the Border Patrol. Tell me about that.'

It surprised Askins. It was the last subject he was expecting. McMann hadn't mentioned Keel for weeks now. And it had been weeks since he had been given instructions to send more money to Sheriff Cole to be passed along to his brother Tully so as to continue making Keel's life as hellish as possible.

'Well, I know he was kidnapped by Apaches when he was four or five years old after they butchered his family,' Askins said, and went into as much detail as he knew, adding also what he knew about Stew Ormond raising him until Keel went trail-herding.

'He had a good rep as a gunfighter and lawman when he joined the Patrol ... and he *was* good, boss. Good tracker, good shot, and good at survival. We got word that Stew Ormond, leadin' an unofficial army troop south of the border, had gone missing around Durango. Word was some bandidos had either killed him or kept him to amuse themselves with.'

'You mean torture,' McMann dropped in, showing a deep interest in what his bodyguard was saying.

Askins nodded. 'They could be worse than Apaches, them *mestizos*, when they wanted to. Well, we were all set to hit a bunch of *contrabandistas* when Keel up and quit. Just rode out with a pack mule and plenty of ammo. We all knew he was heading for Durango.'

McMann frowned. 'Could he do that? Just quit the Patrol?'

'Well, it *was* kind of like deserting the army under fire and I tell you, the captain was mighty riled. He'd been counting on Keel tracking down these gun-runners . . . anyway we set off after 'em, had some luck and cornered them at the hand-over.' Askins finished his drink, twirled the empty glass hopefully between his fingers but McMann only gestured impatiently for him to continue. The bodyguard sighed. 'Things went kind of wrong for us . . . there was the son of a high Mex official involved in the gun deal. We didn't know about him, of course, and when they started shooting, we mixed it with 'em, cut down five, one of whom was — '

'The son of the high-ranking official! But what about Keel, Joel? He's my interest.'

'Coming to that, boss. We knew we were in trouble over this kid being shot down: we were below the border unofficially into the bargain. So the captain said to hell with it. 'Keel quit us. If we'd had him with us, we'd have known who was in the deal. He won't survive them bandits in their own bailiwick, so he can take the blame. Anyone asks, Keel got trigger-happy and smoked the Mexican kid. All right?' . . . It was all right with us. If a dead man was blamed our hides'd be safe.'

McMann drew on his cigar and gestured to Askins to renew their drinks. 'Obviously, Keel wasn't dead at all . . . '

Askins shook his head as he swallowed some more of the fine whisky. 'No. The loco son of a bitch rode into the *bandidos* camp and shot his way out with Stew Ormond who was in a pretty bad way. His mount was hit and he lost his pack mule. They headed into the Sierras and damn if he didn't beat them Mexes at their own game. He outsmarted and out-ran 'em, got back to the States, crossing at Del Rio. Found out he was a wanted man and an embarrassment to the government so he went into hiding. Took old Stew with him — but he didn't need to. Turned out the Mex kid had been kicked out by his old man, anyway, and he didn't care whether he was dead or not. So he wasn't wanted after all.'

McMann's thoughts seemed far away. 'You have to admire the man, Keel, I mean,' he said only half-aloud.

'Loyalty, honour, bravery, he has all three. I think I'd like a man like that on my side.'

Askins felt a shaft of pique. 'Well, he *ain't* on your side, boss: he's agin you. But you've beat him an' no one else has.'

McMann shook his head. 'No, Joel, that's the problem. *No one has beaten Keel!* From Cole's report he's as defiant as ever. They've tried everything and still he won't break!'

He smashed a hand onto the edge of the table, spilling his drink, but ignored it. 'All right, Joel,' he said, mouth pulled tight. 'That'll be all for now. I have a slightly better picture of the kind of man we're up against now. I need to give the matter some more thought, a lot more.'

'You're still gonna bother about him then, boss?'

'You should know better than to ask! Damnit, Joel, don't you see? The man's thumbing his nose at me!'

Askins shook his head, plainly puzzled.

'No, boss, I don't. I mean, you made sure he'll be on that chain-gang for five years! No man's ever lasted that long down there!'

'Now I wouldn't lay any bets that Keel couldn't out-last whatever hell they think up for him, but that's not the point. I'm used to quick results and I'm damn well not getting them.'

'Well, I guess I could ride on down and crowd this Tully Cole a little harder . . . '

'No. I can see we've approached this wrong. I simply didn't realize the kind of man I was dealing with. You leave it with me, Joel. That's all. Good night.'

* * *

Later, lying in bed beside Della, McMann swore softly under his breath. But it disturbed the woman and she turned towards him.

'What's wrong, Shell? You're very restless. Usually after we — '

'Go to sleep!' he snapped.

116

But she wouldn't leave it. She wanted him in a good mood tomorrow because she wanted to go to St Louis to see an old friend. 'It's Keel, isn't it?' she asked with unusual perception. 'He's still getting under your skin, isn't he?'

She felt him go very still and she sucked in a sharp breath: had she made a mistake? Had she said the wrong thing?

Then, surprisingly, in a quiet, even voice, he said, 'Yes, he is still getting under my skin.'

'Well, he's in your hands now, Shell, even though he's way down south on that Texas chain-gang. You control his destiny through the Coles. You can do whatever you like with him.'

'You'd think so, wouldn't you? But — *I can't break the son of a bitch!* He takes whatever is handed out and comes back for more! I see that as total defiance and I will not be defied by anyone!'

She hesitated, but, misled, perhaps, by his being so candid with her, she said, 'Maybe he *can't* be broken, Shell.

There are men like that — Oh!'

She gave a small cry as he literally kicked her out of bed and she thudded to the cold floor.

'Get out!' he hissed.

Shaken, clawing her way to her feet by the bedclothes, she said in a shaky voice, 'But this is my room!'

'In *my* house! Now get out — find somewhere else to sleep tonight. And every other night until I decide you can come back. *Go on! Leave me alone, you tactless bitch!*'

Della fled.

McMann's mood wasn't improved the next morning when a sober-faced Askins handed him a telegraph message.

McMann, eating alone at the breakfast-table, snatched it ill-manneredly and his eyes actually bulged in their sockets as he read Andy Cole's words.

Regret inform you Keel escaped Three Creeks two days ago. Posse hunting him in Warbonnets. Early capture expected.

Askins moved uncomfortably as McMann continued to stare at the message form. ''Early capture', my ass!'

'Want me to go down there and run things our way, boss?'

McMann looked up slowly — and Askins was astonished to see the man was smiling.

'Now that's a fine suggestion, Joel! Except we'll *all* go down and run things the way *I want them*!' He shook the yellow form. 'This couldn't have come at a better time . . . '

★   ★   ★

Keel chose a day when the heat was heavy and he knew the snakes would be hunting the shade under the brush. He had been doing extra work in the stables before breakfast — an added 'incentive' thought up by Tully Cole. Part of his job was washing down the warden's mount and bathing the saddle sores which still had not healed, or, rather, had recurred after healing.

119

This meant using water laced with Epsom salts so as to help dry-out the weeping sores and he kept some aside and, when cleaning up — the lazy guards didn't follow him into the cleaning area — he poured the remains of the water into the hounds' dishes.

It was so hot the dogs came over immediately and began lapping up the water. The saline taste was to their liking, but as the prisoners were being marched out to the road work-area, Keel smiled faintly to himself as he heard the endless howling and yapping of the hounds. Someone said they'd glimpsed the dog pound and two prisoners had been ordered to get it cleaned up as it was heavily soiled.

'Them hounds're shittin' razor-blades,' the man had chuckled. 'They won't be doin' no chasin' anyone today . . . '

Keel was given a stick with an L-shaped blade nailed to the end. The lower part was sharpened and the brush and weeds were cleared by rhythmic swinging of the stick, the blade cutting on both sides. Back and forth, back and forth . . .

It was a Mexican innovation, designed to save effort, and it worked well, though some of the heavier bushes had to be chopped with a hand axe. The guard carried this tool and only brought it to a prisoner who needed to use it.

Keel signalled that he had struck a tough brush and needed the tomahawk. He was happy to see Burl Becker plodding down the slope, billy in one hand, small axe in the other. Only the road guards carried pistols and rifles: keeping the 'ganger' guards unarmed was a safety measure as once, a long time ago, a prisoner had snatched a guard's pistol and shot him dead.

When Becker was still a few yards away, Keel grabbed the brush, trying to loosen it in the parched soil. Suddenly, he yelled and jumped back, deliberately stumbling, grabbing at his ankle as he fell.

'*Snake!*' he yelled, terror in his voice as he rolled about, leg bent. 'Got me on the leg!'

There had been four sightings of rattlers already that morning and men working nearby hurriedly moved away, staring as he rolled about, calling for someone to help him.

Becker paused, looking for the reptile. Ever suspicious, he tossed the tomahawk back up to the road-way before approaching the moaning Keel, calling to the road guard that he would take care of things here. The guard waved and yelled at the other prisoners to keep working: snakebite was of little concern to the guards. It was usually fatal, anyway, and that meant one less hardcase to worry about.

'Where'd it get you?' Becker growled, grabbing at Keel's shoulders, crouching over the prisoner, still sceptical.

Keel, shivering, pointed to his dirt-caked ankles, gasping, eyes bulging in mounting terror.

While Becker roughly grabbed his

manacled ankles and examined the flesh, Keel lifted his right hand to his mouth. He had scraped soap from the hard fragment prisoners used after the day's work, filling the cavity under his fingernails. Now he rubbed those fingernails along his bottom teeth, gouging out the caked soap into his mouth. It mixed with his saliva and he began to froth — one of the signs that the snake poison was rapidly travelling through his body.

'I can't see no bite!' snapped Becker and started when he looked up and saw the foam on Keel's lips.

'Under — the — under the — manacle!' Keel gasped and added a realistic gurgle.

Becker was alarmed now: orders were that Keel could be beaten and ill-treated constantly, but only up to a certain point. He was never to be crippled so that he couldn't work and any guard who beat him badly enough to kill him would answer directly to Tully Cole.

Becker fumbled at his keys, unlocked the manacles and brushed away the dirt from the chronic sores, leaning close to study the flesh.

'Damned if I can see where . . . '

Keel lifted the leg irons by their linking chain and smashed the heavy cuffs across the back of Becker's bent head. The man grunted and sprawled across Keel's legs. He kicked free and hit Becker again with the irons, and then he was scrabbling into the brush on all fours.

Men who had witnessed the faked attack had stopped work, but began again quickly even as the carbine guard started back along his track on the edge of the roadway. Burl Becker lay still, his head in a pool of blood . . .

Keel hoped he wouldn't come across any rattlers but knew that the workers and the noise he was making would likely drive them away ahead of him. He had gone twenty yards before he heard a yell behind him and then a rifle blasting. He dropped flat, panting, almost throwing-up at the taste of the foul soap, spitting out as much as he could. He didn't hear where the bullets went but the guard might have only been firing warning shots to alert the other guards that there was an escape attempt in progress.

Keel jumped up and made a wild, zigzagging dash through head-high brush. Any prisoners nearby moved aside or kicked up as much dust as they could: any man loco enough to try to escape was eligible for their help. A little of themselves seemed to go with the man making his run, even if they knew damn well he would never make it.

Keel heard the rifles banging behind. Bullets spat around him, clipped the brush. He dived headlong, crawled rapidly ahead, swung sharp right and after several yards turned right again and then left. He surged up and found he was only about five yards past the place where he had dived under, but he had confused the guards and they were all shooting far over to his right.

The guns swung back when he was spotted, but he successfully pulled the same manoeuvre again and then came to the first of the creeks. He plunged in, washed out his mouth as he waded across, floundered up the bank and into the heavier brush beyond. It was higher and thicker and gave way to small trees.

He was almost through them, approaching the second, bigger creek when he heard the shouts. He smiled: at least he wouldn't be hearing the baying of the hounds, not with the scouring their bowels had suffered.

The creek was deeper and he had to swim partway. It exhausted him: the lousy prison diet and constant work had done little for his general fitness. Keel floundered under a bush and lay there, gagging and panting from his efforts. He tensed when he heard the guards on the bank he had just left.

'Where *is* that bastard?' one man growled. 'Judas, you wouldn't think he could make it this far, after the hell they put him through back at camp!'

'Well, we better find him, that's all I know,' his companion answered. 'Tully'll castrate us if we let him get away.'

'He'd be the first to do it if he did!'

'Shut up and keep lookin'! The others'll be here soon and you can bet Tully himself'll be along. Be nice if we can hand him Keel, still alive.'

'Christ, yes!'

He heard them smashing at the bushes with their rifle butts and his hand closed over a rock. But they moved downstream, the direction most escapees took, trying to clear the heavy timber of the foothills that led into the rugged Warbonnets.

Keel hoped no one would remember that the Warbonnets were where he had grown-up.

*   *   *

It was mid-afternoon before he reached the very edge of the mountains. He was bleeding from several scratches and his ankles were torn and bloody, his legs shaking with fatigue. The ragged clothes had been torn even more and he was thirsty despite having drunk deeply before leaving the creeks' area.

The searchers were all over the place, but by luck or design he had managed to be somewhere else when a frantic Tully Cole — having taken charge of the search personally — screamed to change direction or go back and search somewhere they had looked at previously.

Keel was moving slowly now and he stopped long enough to stare at the sun's angle, watch the slow movement of the afternoon shadows, and so work out his approximate position.

He was a long way from where he wanted to go but at least he was now in the wild fastnesses of the Warbonnets and he felt more confident. There was still a taste of soap in his mouth and gullet and this gave him a queasiness in the belly which actually worked for him: he didn't feel in the least hungry, with his belly fighting the foul taste of the soap.

It was an illusion, he knew, and decent food was high on his agenda. But water was the first priority: no use a thirsty man gorging on food: it would only dehydrate him further.

There were hidden Indian tanks or springs in these hills and he knew where some were. But that was in the southern part and he was a long way north of the area yet. There were signs to look for, but he couldn't spend time on that this close to where the searchers were. They would move in on the foothills before dark so he would have to be a long way from here by then . . .

★   ★   ★

Tully Cole was almost beside himself and swore constantly, filthy meaningless epithets. His horse's flanks were bloody from his raking spurs and his men gave him a wide berth. Then, late in the afternoon, Andy Cole turned up with a small posse from town.

'How in *hell* did this happen, Tull?' demanded the sheriff.

'Keel,' Tully answered succinctly. 'Faked snakebite and near-killed Becker. Son of a bitch might die yet — hope he does!'

'Well, you cut his sign?' interrupted Andy, still angry.

'Sign? Christ it's all over! But it's damn well hours old before we finally figure out what he's about!'

'Use your damn brains!' the sheriff snapped. 'Judas, the man grew up in these hills! To the south of here! That's the part he knows best and that's where he'll head! Send some men down there — no, I'll take some of my men. You piss around here if you want.'

'Look, this is my deal, Andy! You're outa your bailiwick here.'

The lawman scowled. 'You want me to take my men back to San Antone?'

'No, no, but you ain't gonna take over! This deal's mine! I gotta do this. My job's on the line!'

'I know it is — which is why I'm tryin' to help you out. But, you wanta go it alone, you explain it to McMann.'

Tully paled as Andy started to turn his horse. 'He's comin' — here?'

'Bound to. Now, you want help, or not?'

Tully took a deep breath. 'Andy, I *need* your help, Brother! I just ain't thinkin' straight . . . '

Andy frowned as he saw the way Tully was licking his lips. 'Don't you get no ideas of goin' back on the booze!'

Tully looked pathetic. 'Well, I could sure use a drink right now . . . '

* * *

Keel squeezed the damp mud in his ragged shirt and held his parched mouth beneath the rags. Cloudy water came oozing through and he licked it off, ignoring the gritty taste. He twisted the rags tighter, hoping they wouldn't give way because they were sure rotten.

He had seen the greasewood and

elderberry bush growing in a low spot near a patch of salt grass. It was in an otherwise arid-looking area, at the base of a cliff, and he knew there was a good chance of finding water there if he dug down.

He used a piece of deadwood, came to mud over a foot deep and then scooped up handfuls of it, placed it in his shirt and twisted the cloth around it. He had to work hard for his drink but although it tasted terrible and left his throat feeling gritty so that he hawked a lot, it gave him strength.

It was dark now and he had seen the sheriff's posse arrive earlier. Then Andy had ridden off with his men to the south and Keel knew the lawman would be trying to cut him off from that way. OK, he would go south-west. That ought to take him up near the old adobe ruins of the long-abandoned swing-station. It hadn't been used since the end of the war but it would give him shelter, somewhere to rest-up.

His boots were falling apart, stones

working in constantly through the flapping soles, so he took them off and wove himself a pair of crude sandals. The grass soles were thick and would cushion his bleeding feet better than the worn leather. He used a piece of flint to cut the leather uppers from the boots, keeping them for later use. Tomorrow, he would make himself a proper stone knife, chipping out a blade, tree gum dusted with dirt for a handle. Higher up he would find quartz, too, and would be able to use some to make fire, striking sparks from it with another piece of flint.

He kept some of the dead and dried salt grass lying around: he could tease this out for tinder for starting his fire.

Keel looked up at the stars. He would rest a spell, and then start his journey through the Warbonnets towards his destination. Tomorrow he should be able to find some fire-seasoned hickory or ash that he could use to make a bow. Arrow shafts might be harder to find but he could tip them with flakes of flint, use feathers that birds had lost during a moult — if a man knew where to look he could easily find a couple of handfuls of these.

He ate some more elderberries, rationing himself, for he couldn't afford to be struck down by diarrhoea and lose even more moisture from his body.

Well pleased, despite his exhaustion, and the aches and pains of his battered body, Keel curled up near the base of the cliff behind the greasewood and slept.

8

Survival

The special train with McMann's Pullman car attached came into the San Antone siding late on the third night of Keel's escape.

A weary Sheriff Andy Cole met the rich man and his group, surprised to see Della Lorrance was one of them.

'The lady, Mr McMann . . . you ain't thinkin' of bringin' her out into that wild country, are you?'

McMann glanced at Della who looked tight-lipped and not in the best of moods. 'I don't see why not, Sheriff. The lady, as you call her, seems to be harbouring the notion that this Adam Keel is some kind of superman. That he can't be broken — in fact, can't even be recaptured and returned to the Three Creeks prison camp.'

135

'Shell, I didn't say that — I didn't even *mean* that,' the woman said, and Cole knew for sure she wasn't here because she wanted to be, but because McMann wanted her to be here. But McMann ignored her and spoke to Cole. 'But don't you worry about the lady's welfare, Sheriff. You leave that to me. Now what is the situation?'

'He's been on the run for three days. I tried to outguess him, figured he'd make for the southern part of the Warbonnets as he knows that area best, but seems he veered off somewheres along the way. We lost his sign for nigh on a day.'

He saw McMann's frown of disapproval and hurriedly, added, 'But I brought in an Indian tracker, best man I know for the job — a Mescalero they call Copperhead.' He paused and then added, 'Besides which, he hates Keel's guts so I know he'll be really tryin'.'

McMann seemed uncertain. 'Don't like Indians. Got no use for them.'

'Believe me, Mr McMann, we don't

stand a chance without this feller. Keel's better than I ever thought he was and he don't leave any sign worth a damn that we can pick up. But the Mescalero, he's found traces of him and we've got him more or less cornered now in the south-west section. Mighty rugged, and not much water.'

'Food?'

'Enough for a man who knows how to live off the land.'

'And Keel certainly does from what you've been saying.' McMann sounded almost admiring.

Cole looked a little surprised at that and nodded. 'Yeah, but the Mescalero knows where he'll have to go to find grub and water. Even if he can't pick up tracks, he still has a pretty good idea where Keel's gonna finish up each night.'

McMann was silent a spell, ignoring the woman's impatience and leaving the unloading of the gear to Joel Askins to arrange. Curly Sampson and Shorty Fischer were lounging against the siding, cradling rifles in their arms. Cole was a mite uneasy: this looked like a hunting party to him and he didn't want to lose complete control of things. It was important to him that he maintain some authority ... but he wouldn't buck McMann too strongly. Not when there was money to be made: for that he could swallow a little pride if he had to.

'Why does this Indian hate Keel so much?'

They both looked at Della Lorrance, McMann frowning in annoyance, but she set her gaze on the sheriff and Cole shrugged.

'Goes back a long way. When Keel was a lawman he went after some white woman the Apaches had grabbed. Walked into their camp and challenged the man who'd taken her to hand-to-hand combat: winner gets the woman.'

'This Mescalero you speak of — Copperhead — he was the man who took the white woman?' Della asked and Cole nodded.

'Must've been a helluva fight — war-clubs and knives. Seems Keel won — but he didn't kill the Mescalero. Just took the woman and rode out.'

'You mean . . . ' Della struggled to understand what Cole was saying. 'You mean the Mescalero hates Keel because he *didn't* kill him?'

'That's it, ma'am. He seen it as a kind of shame. Would've been better all round if Keel had knocked his brains out when he had the chance. So Copperhead's been a kinda outcast with his tribe ever since.'

'Hasn't he tried to kill him, to even things up?' McMann asked, interested despite himself.

'Sure, he tried, but Keel wasn't about to play by Injun rules when he didn't have to. To get the white woman back for her family, OK, he'd do what he had to. But he sees this as just some private hate between him and the Mescalero. He's shot the Injun twice, an' Copperhead almost died the second time. But he pulled through and soon as he heard

Keel had busted out of Three Creeks, he come a'ridin' into the Warbonnets where we were an' offered his services.'

Della shuddered. 'I don't think I quite understand a hatred like that. It must be so abiding, so cold!'

'No, ma'am — not cold. It's white hot. Has been for all them years, but Injuns like Copperhead are good at controllin' their emotions. And patient . . . He'll kill him if he gets within spittin' distance.'

'No!' snapped McMann, getting everyone's attention. 'No one kills Keel — I just want him kept on the run for a day or so. Make life hell for him, but have this Indian work him down to some place where we can wait in comfort. Then, when he's close, I want to be informed.' He turned and took the big leather gun case from Joel Askins. McMann slapped his hand against the polished hide. 'I will be the one to' write the last chapter in Adam Keel's life . . . understand, Sheriff?'

'I understand, sir, but I dunno that I

140

can go along with it . . . I mean, folk might say all I did was set-up Keel for you to finish him.'

'Well, it'll be true, won't it?' snapped McMann. 'Of course, you and your brother will be paid well to arrange it . . .'

Still Cole hesitated but greed got the better of him. He nodded. 'Sure, Mr McMann, whatever you say. You want to give instructions yourself to the Mescalero? I can have him here by mornin'.'

'I told you — I don't deal with Indians. You make arrangements and, Andy, they had better be fool-proof. I haven't yet tried out my new rifle on a long shot and I want the first time to be — satisfactory.'

Cole nodded. 'It will be, Mr McMann — I guarantee it.'

McMann looked around him as the sheriff moved away beyond the lights of the siding. He studied the faces of Della and Askins and arched his eyebrows.

'Do I detect disapproval . . . ? Dear

me, and I was looking forward to a good night's sleep. Now it seems I'll be tossing and turning all night, worrying about having upset you both.'

His face straightened as he tossed the gun case back to Askins who hurriedly caught it. Then he took Della by the arm and turned her back towards the Pullman.

'Have everything ready by sun-up, Joel. We'll be ready and waiting.'

'Shell, do I have to . . . ?' asked the girl trying to stop, but he propelled her up the steps to the rail car.

'Of course you do, my dear. You have to see for yourself just how mortal Keel is. Can't leave you with the illusion that he's bigger and tougher and — better — than anyone else.'

He climbed up after her and the door slammed shut with a thud.

*   *   *

He had spotted the dust of the posse heading south and another dust cloud

— Tully's own posse — hunting, back and forth behind him, having trouble finding his trail.

Keel figured it was likely Andy Cole heading south — he was the brains of the Cole family. But Keel swung south-west and confused them both.

He made his way into woodland and, as he had hoped, found a place where wildfire had struck and set a patch of trees on fire long ago. There was both ironwood and hickory amongst the burned timber and brush and he chose a stand of the latter to make his bow. Ironwood would be more durable but harder to work when he had no tools as yet. Osage and yew, of course, were the preferred woods for bow-making but the Indians did all right with hickory and ash. He selected his stave and then knapped thumbnail-size pieces from a shard of flint making it large enough to fit his hand. He used this to shave down the stave, tapering it towards both ends, leaving the thicker middle intact for a hand grip.

He knew this was going to take time and holed-up in a deep cleft between boulders that almost closed out the sky above. It was hard work, laborious, not showing a lot of result for the effort he had to put into it. But he wanted a weapon he could use at reasonably long range — he *had* to have such a weapon if he was going up against guns.

Hungry, thirsty and tired, he finished shaping the hickory to his satisfaction, cut notches in the tapered ends to take the string which he had yet to make. Animal tendon was by far the best but he couldn't hope to take any animal large enough to supply him with the length he required until he had the bow functional. So it had to be grass and he climbed out warily, saw only a distant puff of haze that might have been dust 'way to the south. Long grass was handy enough and he gathered what he wanted, retired to his hidey-hole, removed his ragged trousers and began twisting the strands together, rubbing them across his thighs as the squaws had taught him long ago. The joins were easy and not very neat but the cord he produced was surprisingly strong and, when he started out again, he would look for a wild bees' nest, feast on the honey, and then rub some of the wax along the cord for extra strength and to bind the fibres together.

Arrows were going to be difficult — he *had* to have straight shafts and usually the best way to straighten them was over a fire. He had avoided making fire so far but he knew he would have to do it some time . . . but that would be tomorrow. For now, he would travel for a few hours when it was dark before bedding-down for the night.

★　★　★

He had found a place to sleep on the rim of a narrow canyon — and was more than a little surprised to see the posse's dust in the south-west, swinging towards him. It was far distant right now and he might have been mistaken

— maybe some mustangs or deer had been fleeing a mountain lion and raised that dust, but he couldn't take chances.

He had set a snare near a dead log that was lying near a pile of rocks before turning in, using lengths of cord left over from the bow string. Upon rising he found he had snared himself a rockchuck and he ate it raw, not wanting to take time to build a fire now.

He located water easily enough — sucking the dew from the grass and the leaves of bushes and trees — and then he started down into the canyon. He had seen a thicket that looked like chokecherry which always made good hunting arrows and, beyond, a glimpse of some willows. Branches from these could become good arrows, too, but willows also meant water . . . and, usually, reeds, also good for arrows.

It was a long climb down and halfway his stomach rebelled at the raw meat from the rockchuck. That made it more imperative than ever to locate water. It wasn't hard, once he rounded a bend and could see the clump of willows and after slaking his thirst, he cut reeds with his sharpened flint. They would make light fletchless arrows if he fitted flaky flint heads and strengthened the ends for the nock where it would meet the bowstring. Best of all, these were easy to make and he had a dozen in no time at all.

He tried the bow and recovered all his arrows, working out that the maximum distance he could hope to hit a small target — ground squirrel, quail, etc — with any certainty — was about five yards. Which meant some expert stalking . . .

An hour later he had the plucked carcass of a wood-pigeon on a spit above a small smokeless fire in a trench. His stomach tolerated the cooked meat much better and he ate some currants off a bush and washed it all down with water.

He hoped to bring down a bigger animal like a young pronghorn or a doe, so he could use the intestines as a water carrier, but had no luck. And although the canyon gave him food, shelter and water, he could not get a good view of the country so he had to get up on to higher ground.

He made his way out, carrying the cooked meat from a second pigeon, six of his arrows now fitted with feathered fletches, glued in place with some tree sap and gum. It was a long climb and he rested before tackling the mountainside itself: somewhere up there were the remains of the old adobe swing-station and he made this his goal, aiming to be there by nightfall.

He was — and next day, after fitting lengths of straight ironwood into the reeds as foreshafts for his arrows so he could tackle bigger game, he climbed as high as he dared on the crumbling adobe walls and —

'*Goddamnit!*' he said aloud, shading his eyes, straining to make sure he wasn't seeing things.

But, no, it was a definite dust cloud such as half-a-dozen riders would make. Miles back, but coming along his trail. *Now how the hell? Andy Cole wasn't that smart, and he wasn't that good a tracker, either.*

But someone was. Someone who knew these hills, knew he would make for the old ruins for shelter.

'Copperhead!' he breathed. 'They must've hired-on the goddamned Mescalero!'

He waited around, wanting to be sure, but the dust cloud followed his trail into and out of the narrow canyon. And Keel knew damn well he hadn't left sign enough for any white man to see.

So it had to be the Indian.

In the afternoon, he had confirmation of it when he saw the man, well ahead of the posse, hunkered down studying the ground for tracks. He knew the grass sandals would be shedding a little and spotting any of these small pieces would be enough for the Mescalero. Well, if they had Copperhead coming after him, there was only one way to stop that Indian.

He had to kill him.

And about that time he discovered the swallows building their nest with moist mud, gathered his things and set off to follow their flight path . . . this time deliberately leaving just enough tracks to keep the Indian from becoming suspicious.

★ ★ ★

Now here he was, plastered with mud from the shallow water-hole as some barrier against the mosquitoes that came with sundown, waiting with bow and arrow ready-nocked, fitted with a sharp-edged flint head that would slice through flesh like a razor before snapping off. He had set it horizontal to the nock of the arrow, just as the Indians do when hunting a man they intend to kill. This way, the arrow head would slide between the ribs without striking bone and shattering. When they hunted game, because the animals' ribs were vertical, the arrowhead was also fixed vertically, so it could plough deep into the vitals between the ribcage.

Keel was calm. This wasn't the first time he had waited in ambush to kill a man. But he didn't under-estimate the Mescalero — the man was wilderness-smart, stubborn and cunning as his namesake, and as swift and deadly to strike.

But if Keel could only drive that first arrow home . . .

The mosquitoes whined around him, one or two finding small patches of flesh not covered by the mud but he refrained from slapping at them or scratching at the intolerable itch after-wards. Nightbirds called. Something slithered or padded through the brush, disturbing a few dead leaves. He flared his nostrils now and again, quietly sniffing the air.

Nocturnal animals crept down to the mudhole to drink and disappear again, only ever half-seen. He jumped at a crashing sound and held his breath as a young deer of some sort came and stood tentatively testing the air with its nostrils, then suddenly wheeled and crashed away through the brush. He swore under his breath. It had likely found his man-scent and fled in panic. The noise for those few moments could have kept him from hearing any approach by the Indian, or . . . *Judas priest!*

He didn't smell much like a man, not with all the mud plastered on him. Could the animal have picked up the scent of the Mescalero?

The thought crashed home and his heart began to hammer as he started to turn, grip tightening on the bow, his nostrils filling with a smoky, dusty kind of odour, mixed with stale sweat and rancid fat.

'You wait long, Keel?' someone hissed only a few feet behind him.

* * *

There were eight men gathered around the posse's camp-fire, six that Andy

Cole had brought along and Shorty Fischer and Curly Sampson, sent by McMann.

These two sat a little apart from the main group, talking quietly between themselves. Cole scrubbed off his empty tin platter with a handful of sand and walked across.

'We could be in a little trouble,' he said, hunkering down and taking out his pipe from his shirt pocket.

Sampson looked up, mouth all greasy from the venison steak, wiped the back of a hand across his lips and said, 'Not we, pardner, *you*. Shorty an' me are only along to see things go the way McMann wants.'

'Yeah, well, they have been goin' good. The Mescalero's the best tracker in the South-west . . . but he's gone.'

The hardcases stiffened. Shorty Fischer said, 'What you mean — gone?'

Cole puffed his pipe alight before answering, head shrouded in the aromatic tobacco smoke. 'Gone. Din' say nothin', but way I figure him, he's worked out where Keel's headed an' he's gone to wait for him.'

'Well, that's OK,' allowed Curly. 'Figure he can jump Keel an' bring him down? I mean, is he that good?'

Cole puffed away, cleared his throat and spat. 'I think he's good enough to kill the son of a bitch — and that's what bothers me. I think he's gone to kill him.'

There was a brief silence and Curly and Shorty exchanged worried looks.

'He damn well better not!' snarled Sampson eventually. 'McMann don't want Keel dead. *He* wants to finish him himself.'

'Well, Keel and the Mescalero have hated each other a long, long time. If he gets Keel up on the mountain, he'll kill him all right.'

'Then he better not come back to collect his money!' Fischer said.

Andy Cole laughed briefly. 'Money? He don't care about money. He wants Keel's scalp and when he gets it we'll never see him again.'

The two hardcases looked really worried now. 'We got to stop him,' Curly said quietly. 'Christ, if he kills Keel, McMann'll use us as goddamn targets!'

'Well, I dunno where he went. He was eatin' with the rest of us, and then I looked up an' he was — gone. Din' take his horse or his guns, just his scalpin' knife — that's how I know what he's about.'

The hardcases were on their feet now. 'Man, we gotta do somethin'! We gotta stop him!'

'Lots of luck,' Cole said. 'Me, I wouldn't go prowlin' that mountain in the dark with that Mescalero on the loose. He'll know that anyone who comes after him will be tryin' to stop him gettin' to Keel.'

Sampson and Fischer looked mighty worried, pushing their unfinished meal aside now, suddenly no longer hungry. They hurried to their mounts, Curly limping on his wounded leg.

★ ★ ★

It had to be the Mescalero.

The thought burned across Keel's brain as the hissing words fell into the night and he threw himself forward off the rock where he had been crouching, twisting his body in mid-air, loosing off the arrow. He saw the sparks strike from the rock surface and knew he had missed, and smashed his best arrow into the bargain.

Not that it mattered much. He glimpsed a shadow flitting across the stars and then the weight of the Indian smashed him flat and he threw his bow to one side, reaching for his fragile stone knife which he wore on his upper arm, held in place with a plaited armlet of grass. Starlight glinted off steel as Copperhead slashed at him. He felt the slight tug as the honed blade sliced through his ragged shirt and laid open his flesh across his ribs.

'Not fast for you, Keel!' hissed the Mescalero and Keel knew he was going

156

to be slowly cut to ribbons before the Indian would finish him off.

'But fast for *you!*' Keel gritted, feeling the blood flowing across his ribs as he slashed backhand with his flint knife.

It caught the Indian unawares and Keel felt the jar as the stone blade hit the flat, ugly face and cut the cheek open to the bone, sliced deep into the bridge of the aquiline nose and just missed the eye.

It was a bad wound, but the Indian made no sound apart from a barely audible grunt as he staggered back. Keel went after him, but wrenched his lean body aside as the knife sliced edge-up, trying to cut his stomach open. He smashed down with his left fist, hitting the Indian's muscular arm, hammering it aside. He swung the flint knife, turned it so that the tree-gum handle, protruding past his palm, would take the Indian in an eye and gouge it. The Mescalero moved like a snake, fast and weaving, and the hilt slid off his greasy hair.

And then his thick arms were about Keel and he pulled him in close and brought up a knee. Keel wrenched and took most of the blow on his thigh but some of it crushed his genitals and he moaned sickly, trying to double-up so as to ease the pain. But Copperhead held him, tried again with the knee and this time Keel managed to trap the leg between his.

Keel clenched his muscles tight, holding the Indian one-legged, writhed, and threw him off-balance. They crashed to the ground and rolled and the Mescalero grunted again, tried to head-butt Keel and, when he missed, put up one powerful, clawed hand and grabbed the white man's throat.

'This time — *you* — die!'

Keel didn't waste breath. He snapped his head forward so that his forehead smashed across Copperhead's nose. It broke but the grip on Keel's throat didn't weaken. The Indian roared and flung Keel around, holding him at arm's length with the stranglehold, swinging the knife with his other hand, slicing at Keel's left ear.

Desperately, Keel spat into the broad face and the Mescalero hesitated a fraction of a second, shocked, and Keel ducked his head, fastened his teeth onto the man's bloody nose. Copperhead roared again and wrenched his head wildly, striking madly with the knife. Keel felt the blade open a gash on his left shoulder, wrenched his head back, tearing at the nose, spitting blood and flesh.

The Mescalero's legs buckled briefly and Keel snapped up his knee and felt it smash into something soft beneath the man's buckskin trousers. Copperhead sagged further and Keel smashed the strangling hand from his throat, kicked the man in the belly and broke free. The Indian rolled backwards and Keel lurched forward, stomped on the knife hand. He ground down and his sandal crumbled and almost tripped him. But he dropped knee-first onto the barrel chest and drove an elbow into the bloody face. Copperhead slumped but twisted away, kicking out.

He groped for his fallen knife, half on his belly, and Keel wrenched the man over, straddled his broad back and locked his hands under the blood-slippery chin. He fumbled the grip and Copperhead snapped at his hand with his big teeth. Keel locked the hands in place an instant later, rammed a knee against the man's spine and leaned his weight back. The Mescalero hissed and wrenched and fought and almost threw Keel, but the white man held on, teeth bared, his arms creaking with effort. His knee pushed and his locked hands pulled. The Indian's efforts grew slower, weaker, and suddenly there was a sound that Keel knew he would never forget as long as he lived and the Indian slumped, kind of folded the wrong way — Keel flung him aside, fell sprawling and lay there, stomach heaving, air whistling and wheezing in his throat.

He had no thoughts. There was no

elation. It was something that had had to be done and he had *done* it. Now, with a little luck, he could shake the posse and stay free in the Warbonnets until they got tired of looking.

But, as he sat up slowly, he knew there was always McMann. The posses might eventually give up, but Shelby McMann wouldn't.

Not until Adam Keel was dead — with McMann's long-distance bullet in his broken body.

9

Stalker

Curly Sampson figured he was lost.

He should have listened to Sheriff Cole and stayed back in camp instead of setting off in an attempt to head-off the damn Indian who was out to kill Keel.

But he knew he and Shorty had to do *something*: otherwise McMann would have *their* scalps. The hills were kind of creepy at night and there wasn't enough moon to be sure the shadows weren't closing in on a man. He had become separated from Shorty Fischer halfway up the slope. There was a fold in the hills that had somehow gotten between them and now he couldn't find it again.

He decided to make camp for the night — camp? Well, all he did was spread his blankets and groundhitch and hobble his horse. Curly Sampson was too damn tired for anything else.

Come morning, he was no better off. He didn't know where he was, couldn't locate the fold because of the line of timber in the way. There was no sign of the Indian or Shorty, and, to make it worse, there was a damn mist you could cut with a knife.

He decided to head on down at an angle, leading his horse, although it would have been better for him to ride and trust to the mount's instinct to find a safe way through the mist. He fell several times, heard a couple of sounds that made the hair prickle on the back of his neck and unsheathed his rifle, jacking a shell into the breech.

'Shorty?' he called tentatively, his low voice seeming to be thrown back at himself by the blanket of mist. He cleared his throat and called more loudly, '*Shorty!*'

No answer. But his call was heard . . . not by Shorty Fischer, though . . .

Keel was moving cautiously through the mist. He was wearing the dead Indian's clothes now and they didn't fit very well but were more substantial than the old prison rags. The shirt stank and while large enough in the chest, was too short in the sleeves. The buckskin trousers, too, were short but Copperhead had been wearing half-leg moccasin boots, the soft tops folded over. They fitted well enough and Keel pulled up the folded sections and they covered the short legs of the trousers.

He moved silently, groping his way over broken rocks, the Mescalero's scalping knife in its hide sheath rammed into his belt. He had lost some arrows during the fight but had five serviceable ones, the best already nocked into his bow string. He came to what seemed like a natural drain and he found several little pools of water trapped amongst the smooth-worn pebbles. He drank, clambered up the cleft on all fours and was just straightening so he could see over the edge when he froze.

A man's voice echoed dully through the heavy layers of mist, calling *Shorty!* The mist gave him no certain direction, but he knew it was likely Curly Sampson doing the calling. And that was fine with him . . .

The man called again, more sharply and louder, and there was a slight touch of worry that brought a cold smile to Keel's lips as he eased up, raising the bow. He saw the shadowy form and the horse behind the man. Curly was side-on and his rifle clipped a rock, the metallic sound warning Keel. Well, he didn't want any gun shots: the rest of the posse could be scouring the mountain.

The string came back alongside his face and when it touched the tip of his nose, he held the draw, shifted aim slightly as Curly turned and then released. There was the usual quiet *thrum* of the string, followed swiftly by the zip of the arrow and a soft sound as it struck home, the flint head slicing between Curly's ribs, deep into his lungs and heart before emerging under his right arm.

Any scream was cut off by the swift deadliness of the arrow destroying his vital organs and his body tumbled down the slope, the rifle clattering a little. Keel moved aside as Sampson dropped into the cleft, leapt out and snatched at the trailing reins of the horse. But the animal was frightened, by both the smell of fresh blood and the shadowy apparition that came running towards it. It wrenched away with a low whinny and ran out of reach.

Keel swore as he heard it running and sliding down the slope. He turned back to Sampson's rifle and then climbed down to the dead man. He took his hat, tobacco, clasp-knife, six-gun rig and trousers. The riding boots were a little large so he left them, preferring the Mescalero's moccasins. While Keel felt better now that he had firearms and more serviceable clothes, he still wished he had managed to catch that horse. However, he kept the bow and remaining arrows. They might be crude, but they were silent and deadly.

If he ran across any more of the posse, he still didn't want any shooting that would draw them to him.

As the sun rose, it burned away the mists and Keel made his way down to a fold in the hills that he knew would lead him to the lower, southern foothills, which was where he wanted to go. As vision improved, he found the tracks of the runaway horse and decided to follow them as they led towards the ridge and the fold where he had been heading anyway.

He moved quietly, seeing a couple of deer that he could have brought down with the rifle but he had to let them go. A rifleshot here would carry for miles, slapping back and forth between the hills and from the sheer rock faces. His belly growled as he slid a little way over the ridge and then he saw Shorty Fischer . . .

The man was in a clearing below him, on foot, his mount standing by with trailing reins while Fischer examined the horse that Keel had been following. It had found the other man unerringly and Shorty examined the saddle and hide closely, but Keel knew he wouldn't find any blood there to tell him what had happened to Sampson.

Keel didn't give him a chance, or, about as much chance as Shorty had given old Stew Ormond . . . which was to say none at all.

The arrow took the hardcase just under the left shoulder and burst out through his chest while the startled man was looking down so that he actually saw the flint head emerge and a foot of the crude shaft, glistening with his blood. He got off a scream that lifted the short hairs at the back of Keel's neck and it echoed through the clearing.

Keel moved swiftly and as quietly as

he could: he didn't aim to scare the horses this time. They were skittish, but when he appeared, they seemed to relax, no doubt reassured by his appearance in Sampson's hat and trousers. Shorty was dead by now and Keel bent over him, examining his arrow critically: flint-head still attached, shaft unsplintered.

He nodded to himself: he had made a better job of it than he had thought.

★   ★   ★

Joel Askins came out of the large tent and lifted his field-glasses to his eyes, focusing on the figure he could see in the distance approaching the camp.

There was heat-haze, of course, and some dust that distorted the man and his animals at first, and then Askins stiffened, stared a little longer, lowered the glasses and glanced back over his shoulder into the main part of the tent.

McMann was sitting in a canvas

chair, reading, his shiny new Remington close to hand, also a small folding table set up with bottle and glasses. Della Lorrance was sitting up on a collapsible bed, writing letters. Both McMann and the girl glanced up as Askins entered slowly, still holding his field-glasses.

'Visitor,' he said shortly and McMann's brow creased slightly as he waited for more specific information. 'I think it's the sheriff.'

'Ah!' McMann said, sitting up straighter in his chair. 'About time he was bringing us some news of Keel.'

Askins hesitated briefly before saying, 'I — I'm not sure why he's coming, boss, but he's leading a horse and it looks to me like it's got two dead men roped across it.'

McMann surged upright. 'By God, if Cole's let that blasted Indian kill Keel . . . '

He stormed outside, snatching the glasses from Askins' hands as he did so. The girl swung her legs off the bunk and started out as Joel followed McMann.

McMann swore as hc stared through the glasses. 'Can't see anything. He's got them covered with a blanket.'

'He'll be here in about ten minutes,' Askins said quietly, but McMann was too jumpy now, had been raw-edged for days since making this camp, waiting for Cole to keep his word that he and his men would drive Keel down out of the hills to a certain part of the distant hogback rise that McMann had already set his new rifle's range for.

Now ... well, if Cole was only delivering Keel's body, Askins wouldn't want to be that sheriff for anything in this world.

'Go give our guest some more comfort, Joel.'

Askins looked startled. 'But — '

'Do it!'

Askins went to one of the smaller tents, got a bottle and entered another where Tully Cole lay on a bed. The man was unshaven, dishevelled, and reeked of whiskey. He had a foolish, loose look on his face. Askins curled a lip and held out the bottle.

'Stay outa sight till you're called.'

Tully grabbed the bottle, starting to work out the cork. 'Wha'ever you say, Joel, ol' pard — care for a snifter?'

'Not after your mouth's touched the neck.' Joel stabbed a finger at the bleary-eyed man. 'Do as you're told and there'll be more of that rotgut: gimme trouble, and . . . '

Tully held up one hand in acknowledgement but didn't take the bottle away from his mouth.

★ ★ ★

Sheriff Andy Cole dismounted stiffly, red-eyed and wary as McMann waited, arms folded, face grim.

Cole whipped the blanket off the two bodies on the second horse and Della said tightly, 'Isn't that Shorty's mount?'

'Yes'm — an' that body wearin' clothes is the man himself. The nekked one is Curly.' The sheriff glanced at McMann. 'They both been killed by bow and arrow. Hoss wandered into camp early this mornin', the bodies already roped to it.'

'The Indian did this?'

'Keel, I reckon. They're rough-made arrows, reed with dogwood foreshafts, flint heads. Pretty good, mind, and they sure done the job, but they ain't up to Injun standard. 'Sides, we found the Mescalero higher up with his back broke.'

McMann smiled. 'Keel is turning out to be a truly worthy adversary. Where is he now?'

'We've lost him for the moment, but the sonuver's got rifles and six-guns now.'

McMann's eyes narrowed. 'I hope you're not telling me that this means he has a better chance of getting away.'

Cole moved uneasily. 'Well, he's got Curly's hoss and this is the neck of the woods he knows best. It won't be as easy as we'd hoped to haze him down in this direction, Mr McMann. Gonna take a lot of work — '

'I'm not interested in your difficulties! I paid you to do a job and I want it *done*!'

'The men are tired — *I'm* tired. Keel's out-lastin' us all . . . I dunno if the men want to keep on, Mr McMann. They got familes, an' truth is, they're kinda scared of the way Keel took care of that Mescalero and two of your top hardcases.'

'I suppose they want more money,' McMann said tightly.

'Yeah, that might do it.' Cole tried to sound as if the idea had just occurred to him.

And then McMann knew that this was just a shakedown: the posse wanted more money and had grabbed at this chance to milk him of a few more dollars. *Like hell!*

'*Joel*! Damn you, get out here!'

Askins came out with Tully Cole, half-carrying the man who was starting to sing some unrecognizable song, lurching and staggering. Andy Cole stiffened, his jaw sagging. Then his eyes bulged and his face darkened as he spun towards McMann.

'Who give Tull likker?' he asked very quietly.

McMann merely stared and Cole dropped a hand to his gunbutt, glaring now at Joel. 'Was it you, Askins? Christ, the trouble I had gettin' him off the booze before!'

He strode forward and slapped Tully across the face, shook the man as Askins stood there silently, watching.

'Tully! Damn you! What are you *doin'*, for *Chris'sakes*? Aw, Judas wept, man, look at you! Just as bad as a couple of years ago . . . '

'H-howdy, Andy. They fired me from Three Creeks, Brother! I was kinda — lost. Wandered in here an' Mr McMann, he sure knows when a man needs comfort . . . '

Cole's eyes blazed at Askins, then he swung towards McMann. 'Damn you, McMann! Why'd you do it? Why? He's weak; I just manage to keep him sober and now . . . '

'Whatever is wrong with him is his own fault, Sheriff. I merely offered something to ease his pain.'

'Don't sound like you!' Andy gritted. 'Bein' considerate!'

'Oh? Saying what you *really* think for once, are you, Sheriff?' McMann said calmly. 'Actually, I suspected you and your men might try to prise more money out of me, blackmail me into paying up or they would abandon the hunt for Keel. Now, you *make* them hunt him down! Make them haze him out onto the ridge! Make them stick to their bargain! In return, I'll see what I can do about getting your brother's job back . . . and, perhaps — er — straightened out a little.'

'You cold-hearted bastard! You got him fired in the first place, I wouldn't wonder. Then reduced the poor sonuver to *that*, just so's you can take a long shot at Keel? You're crazy, you son of a bitch! You know that? Got to be!'

'Joel!' McMann said in a deceptively quiet voice and Askins stepped forward.

Cole spun towards him dragging at his six-gun. Askins' hands came up holding a blazing Colt in each fist and Andy Cole was flung backwards by the bullets and went down into the dust, legs kicking briefly as the gunfire dwindled. Della gasped and stepped back involuntarily. Tully blinked, shocked by the suddenness of the violence and seeing his brother's bloody body lying almost at his feet. He dropped to his knees and cradled Andy's head against his thighs.

'Aw, Andy, *Andy*! I — never meant to let you down, l'il brother, never meant . . . couldn't help it . . . I . . . '

Della was white and shaking. 'Shell. This is horrible! What're you going to do with Tully now? Obviously he can't cope. He needs some expert help . . . '

McMann's eyes were cold. 'I don't believe he's my responsibility.' He gestured grandly with one hand. 'But

— if your mothering instinct is rearing its head . . . '

She gasped. 'You're really a true son of a bitch, aren't you, Shell?' She hardened her voice and tilted her jaw at him. 'Very well, if you won't help him — I've had enough of this anyway. I'm going back to San Antone and I'll take Tully with me.'

McMann's cold expression didn't change. 'Don't stop at San Antone, my dear, just keep right on going.' As she stood there, shocked into immobility, Tully sobbing, rocking back and forth as he nursed his dead brother, McMann turned to Askins. 'Joel, get back to that posse and whip them into shape. I want to see Keel up on that ridge by this time tomorrow.'

'Whatever you say, boss,' Askins replied reloading his Colts. 'Better fine-tune your new rifle — you're gonna be needing it.'

'I'd better.'

10

Warbonnet

Keel was in trouble.

There seemed to be men crawling all over the Warbonnets, armed men waiting whichever way he went. Or *tried* to go. He figured McMann must have called in the posse from Three Creeks whose members Keel thought he had lost long since. They were coming down on him from behind, out of the timber, closing in and pushing him down into the lower foothills — where Andy Cole's posse from San Antone was ready and waiting for him.

He made a mistake, a bad one, which almost cost him his life. He had assumed that the men behind were Andy Cole's posse and had run Curly's big roan down through the hill folds into the more open country, figuring to make a dash through it and into the tangle of canyons that lay beyond. Once in there no one would find him, not even an Indian.

And that was when Cole's posse came up out of a draw, guns blazing. They were trying to shoot his horse out from under him and he reckoned McMann wanted him alive. Likely so he could use him as a human target for that damn Remington rolling-block of his. It would be a long shot, but that was what McMann wanted: he was one of those men who would spot a woodchuck or a ground squirrel half a mile away and get a big kick out of picking it off with his fancy rifle and 'scope sight. The bullet would blast the little animal into bloody bits of hide and shattered bone, but McMann would get a real kick out of it. A successful long-distance shot counted more for him than the target.

Keel had heard there were men like that, using the more modern firearms that could reach out to around one mile, and knock an animal dead, big or small. It wasn't Keel's notion of what a *real* hunter ought to be doing — and he liked the idea even less when *he* was to be the target.

But with posse lead singing about his ears, kicking dust fountains across the slope, above and below him, Keel swung the roan downslope and rammed home his heels. The horse didn't much like the idea of going down such a steep grade so fast but it reacted instinctively to the touch of his heels and bounded forward. Keel threw his weight back in the saddle, long legs in the stirrups going forward and angled straight down, using the reins to swing the roan in a kind of rhythmic zigzag. But he changed the manoeuvre after a few yards, weaving randomly before the shooters could get used to his rhythm.

Some lead came close and then he yanked hard right, bringing the horse's head around brutally, a snorting whinny of protest exploding from it. He raced for the gap between some boulders and two bullets ricocheted from the left hand rock, *zinging* across to the opposite boulder, spraying him with rock chips.

He was into the boulder-field and starting to slow when two riders came out from behind large rocks, higher up the slope, within ten yards of him.

Their rifles whipcracked simultaneously and he felt the roan stagger, heard it whinny again, and then he hauled left and got behind another rock. He quit saddle in a leap, taking the rifle with him out of its scabbard. Legs folding under, Keel shoulder-rolled two yards down-grade, flopped onto his belly between two smaller rocks. The men up above had to bring their horses around the big boulders to get a shot at him.

But they never did get off any more aimed shots. Keel's rifle cracked three times and both men went back and over their saddles, one striking the rounded rock and spilling off so that he rolled down almost in front of Keel. The other man was hurt and clutched at his side, but made a grab for his six-gun anyway.

He managed to take two steps before Keel brought him down. Keel jacked a fresh shell into the breech, reached out to the dead man in front of him and dragged him a little closer. He turned the body towards him, recognizing him as a man from San Antone he had seen hanging around the Alamo saloon and occasionally working the corrals at the rear of the livery. Someone said he had once strangled a whore, but as far as Keel knew the man hadn't made any undue trouble in town. Well, he'd never make trouble of any kind now.

The other one he didn't know for sure but thought he was a rider from one of the trail herds, likely trying to make a quick stake. He felt nothing for either of them: greed had motivated them, not civic duty, so as far as he was concerned it was them or him.

And he had no intention of it being *him*, now or later.

The roan was body-hit, down on its

side, when he went back to it. He shot it to put it out of its misery, selected a long-legged claybank from the dead men's mounts and quit that part of the slope just as the posse, now mounted, started up towards the boulder field.

They weren't wasting any time. They wanted him quickly and from what he could judge, they were trying to force him more southerly than he was heading. There were some low ridges over there, pretty much open country.

Giving a good line of fire for any kind of long shot.

★　★　★

Along the trail back to San Antone, Tully sobered-up. Not slowly, but suddenly, like a bolt of forked lightning sizzling out of the blue and stunning him briefly.

Della was riding slowly, although she was in the lead and she heard him suddenly curse, hipped in the saddle, and saw him hauling rein on his dun.

The man was staring straight at her but she could see his eyes weren't focused on her.

'What's wrong, Tully?'

He frowned and slowly her words reached him through whatever mental fog clouded his mind. 'Oh, ma'am, I — I recollect you was takin' me in to San Antone . . . '

'Yes, but we have a long way to go yet.'

'I ain't goin',' he said curtly, his voice all gravelly from his drinking. 'Now don't get me wrong, I 'preciate you tryin' to help me, but — well, I feel stone-cold blamed sober of a sudden. An' I know I can't just ride out an' leave Andy back there.'

'They'll bury him, Tully.'

He shook his head. 'No, I shoulda brought him along. I want to bury him. I owe him that. He was my l'il brother, but he looked out for me, got me off the booze a couple years back and into that job at Three Creeks. Sure, it weren't much but we made a little money together here and there over an' above our pay . . . I guess I was a kinda mean bastard, but that's in my nature. Only time I ain't is when I'm drunk, I guess. Then I don't remember much about bein' mean . . . '

'What're you trying to say, Tully?'

'I guess I'm sayin', it's time I stood up for Andy after all the times he's stood up for me.'

'But your brother is dead now, Tully . . . ' Gently, patiently.

'I know that, an' you don't have to talk to me like I'm a five-year-old child! I mighta been kinda stupid . . . when I was drinkin' but right now I'm . . . OK.'

She made herself smile, just a little afraid and not quite knowing why. 'And I'm glad, Tully. Now why don't we keep on to San Antone so we'll be there before dark?'

He shook his head, taking out his six-gun and, although his hands were shaking, he checked the loads expertly enough. He glanced up at her. 'I'm

186

goin' back. I want Andy's body, to lay him to rest proper, an' I want McMann an' Joe Askins.'

'Joel,' she corrected automatically. 'Tully, you can't do it! You'll never get near McMann. Askins will see to that and — well, you won't stand a chance against a gunfighter like him.'

'Mebbe — but I gotta try, ma'am. I know I'm dirt an' have been for a long time, an' Andy weren't no angel, neither, but he done a lot for me and now I gotta try to do what I can for him. I gotta *try!*'

She started to argue with him but soon saw there was no point: his mind was made up. There was a kind of twisted honour in the man. She knew his reputation as a sadistic warden at Three Creeks and had watched him with disgust when he was drunk at the camp, but there was at least the ashes of dignity in him and he had managed to drag them to the surface.

'I wish you luck, Tully,' she said abruptly and lashed at her horse with the rein ends, riding off swiftly.

Tully watched her go and then turned his dun and started back towards McMann's camp . . .

* * *

When he got there, the only one he could see around was McMann himself, although he knew Andre the cook would be busy in his own tent preparing the evening meal for his master.

He looked around for some sign of Joel Askins, knowing the man was never far from his boss, but couldn't see any sign of his horse or the man himself. Didn't matter anyway: both men were going to die before sundown.

Tully left the dun roughly ground-hitched in some brush, checked his gun again, wishing his hands weren't so shaky: what he needed was a steadying drink and the thought had hardly formed before he was making his way silently towards McMann's tent where the man had gone while he watched only a few minutes ago. Yeah, one steadying drink before he put a bullet into the sonuver . . .

He reached the tent flap and McMann was still inside. Tully flung the flap aside and stepped in, gun ready. Shelby McMann, who was rummaging in a briefcase crammed with papers, looked up. His face showed brief surprise but not much.

'I wondered if you'd come back, Tully. Don't worry about your brother. Joel has had his instructions about what to do with the body.'

Tully frowned, disconcerted by McMann's calmness and his words. 'I want to bury him myself.'

'Well, I'm not sure about that. You see, I told Joel to take the body, strip it, and leave it on some rocks near that water-hole just this side of the crest of the humpback . . . I'm hoping it will attract that big mountain cat that is supposed to inhabit the area. I was hoping for a little entertainment — and some ranging shots with my rifle.' He indicated the Remington resting on a folding table. 'While I waited for the men to drive Keel in — rather like a lot of beaters in India, driving the tiger towards the waiting *raj* and his entourage.'

The words confused Tully but something finally got through the turmoil in his head. 'You left Andy out as *lion-bait*!'

McMann shrugged. 'He's only dead meat now, Tully . . . I'm just putting him to one final use.'

An anguished cry was wrenched from Tully and he brought up his Colt — but McMann lifted his rebuilt gold-handled gun stick from where it rested against his left leg and shot him through the middle of the chest.

Tully's eyes flew wide and he swayed. His mouth moved but only guttural sounds and some bright blood came from it as his legs gave way and he collapsed.

Joel Askins appeared in the doorway,

guns out and ready for action. 'All right, boss . . . ?'

'Yes . . . what're you doing back here?'

'Keel's killed three more men, wounded two others — '

'Is he being driven into the area I want?' interrupted McMann and Askins stopped, then nodded. 'Then that's all that matters. Oh, when you go, take Tully with you and put him with his brother. I've rather taken a fancy to the notion of shooting that big cat from here — '

'If he exists.'

'Oh, I think he does. The one thing I'm certain about where Keel is concerned, is that he is not a liar. Now hurry it along, Joel! I'm growing impatient to test the Remington against live prey!'

*　 *　 *

They were closing in on Adam Keel.

He thought he had managed to shake

most of the posse by heading for the canyon country, but he didn't get that far before bullets were ripping air overhead as he put the claybank down a steep slope. There was a good deal of loose scree and as he hipped in the saddle, looking for the gunmen, his weight shifted and the horse snorted, weaved involuntarily and together they went down in a small avalanche of gravel and a huge dust cloud.

He slipped sideways as the claybank lost footing and started to roll. He had no choice but to quit leather with a wild leap and he jarred hard when he hit, tumbling out of control. The world went crazy for a time as he thudded in a series of sprawling somersaults and bright lights exploded behind his eyes as he fought to slow his descent. The horse rolled almost on top of him, legs thrashing, and he wrenched aside desperately to dodge the hoofs. One caught him a glancing blow on the back and he was mighty glad it wasn't full force. But it helped him at the same time.

The impact hurled him on to a part of the slope that had much less scree and he was able to slow down, get some measure of control, although he continued to slide on his back now. The horse was turning as it slid and struck the bottom first, whinnying loudly, spinning full circle, immediately trying to struggle to its feet. Keel managed to grab a bush and stop his own descent although his arms jerked painfully in their sockets. Panting, coughing in the clouds of dust, he pushed upright and staggered to the floundering horse. He climbed into saddle as the animal heaved up, snatched at the horn to keep from falling again.

Then he leaned down, grabbed the trailing reins, talking quietly into the claybank's ear, calming it as he settled back and put a little pressure on the bit. These familiar things helped settle the horse and he kicked with his heels, groping for the rifle, relieved that it hadn't fallen out of the scabbard.

He levered and looked back up the slope. He couldn't see clearly because of the dust he had raised but he heard men shouting and decided to make use of the dust cover.

Keel heeled the claybank again, bringing it to a fast walk rather than a canter, and headed down the draw, hoping to drop out of sight before the men up top were able to see properly. Not that it would matter a great deal because there weren't many places he could go and down the draw was the most obvious one, it being the easiest.

But he didn't care if they guessed which way he went — because he aimed to be waiting for them when they came.

* * *

It was getting on towards sundown when Shelby McMann saw the movement on the hogback and a slinking, belly-dragging shadow that could only be the big cat. At least *nine feet!*

He was sitting in his folding canvas chair and set down the field-glasses on the small table beside his drink. Savouring the moment, he picked up the glass and sipped the malt whisky, rolling it around his tongue before swallowing.

Then he reached for the shiny Remington rifle propped up in a special polished cedar stand. He flicked the personalized butt into his shoulder with a showy but expert movement, settled the cheek-piece and then flipped off the covers of the long German-made telescopic tube sight. The front lens was hooded so that the glass wouldn't flash in the sunlight and he moved the whole weapon as he 'scoped the hogback, looking for the cougar.

'Ah! There you are, you elusive son of a bitch!'

Without taking the rifle from his shoulder, he reached out to the table where the carton of hand-loaded cartridges rested, took one which already had a cross cut into the nose so that it would expand immediately on hitting flesh, and smash its way through bone if necessary.

McMann loaded in automatic motions, keeping his right eye close to the rear lens of the sight, still searching for the cat. It had gone to ground in the deep shadows, no doubt cautiously studying and sniffing the bait. On McMann's instructions, Askins had laid out the naked dead men across two boulders, bending back the bodies so that their wounds were uppermost, giving the best scent of blood and whatever corruption had already started. He smiled as he imagined how the cat must be salivating by now.

He found the cat again, creeping inch by inch towards the baited boulders. This 'scope was so good he could actually see the muscles rippling beneath the tawny hide.

There was an African tribe called the Masai where he had hunted one time. They had a saying that a brave man is frightened three times by a lion: when he first sees its tracks; when he first hears it roar; and when he first sees the lion in the flesh.

'Well, I'm seeing you very well, Mr Cougar, but I'm not in the least frightened. So, as my friend Adam Keel would say, *adios, amigo*! It's time for you to become a *real* legend and that only happens after death!'

He drew in a breath, released a little, finger stroking the finely set trigger, taking up the slack, feeling the first let-off of the beautifully machined metal, and then came the satisfying *thump!* of the rifle recoiling against his shoulder, the blasting thunder of the big .58 calibre bullet being sent on its way . . .

McMann waited for what seemed an age and then smiled as the big cat seemed to be thrown into the air, spinning once before crashing to the ground. He could even see its snarl — or imagined he could anyway.

Then the smile vanished as the

cougar leapt to its feet and ran off towards the rocks and dropped out of sight.

He slammed a hand against the hand-carved walnut stock of the rifle.

'Goddamn! It's shooting low and to the left!'

He had set the cross-hairs squarely on the animal's muscled shoulder but it seemed his lead had struck the sagging, empty belly. The big cat was gut-shot . . .

'Well, suffer, you son of a bitch!' he snarled, shaking a fist impotently towards the ridge. 'Suffer and die in much bloody pain!'

11

Quits!

Keel settled himself on the rim of the narrow draw, the horse hidden amongst the rocks. Behind him rose the small hogback, beyond which stretched the wildest canyon country this side of the Pecos.

He waited, rifle magazine fully loaded, hat pushed back slightly so the brim didn't get in the way of his sighting. The sun was tilting fast into the west now and he picked up a little glare out of the corner of his left eye. But that wouldn't affect his shooting. Normally he shot with both eyes open, but he could shoot just as well with the left eye closed.

The posse would have to come through the narrowest part of the draw and that meant only one rider at a time.

They didn't know this area of the Warbonnets and, in their hurry to get him, they hadn't yet realized the trap he had led them into.

But they were about to find out.

They came in at speed, raising a roiling dust cloud behind them, eager to get to him before sundown, he figured. Two riders tried to get through the narrow gap together, their horses fighting and rearing, scraping off hide against the rocks. The men were shouting and cursing at each other, neither one wanting to pull back.

Keel couldn't find a certain target, they were moving about so much, so, against his grain, he picked one of the struggling horses and shot it through the head.

The shot crashed and echoed up the draw and the mounts were jammed so tightly in the narrow-neck that the dead horse couldn't easily fall. It started down, dragging its rider, who got his leg caught between it and the other man's horse. He screamed and

200

struggled, dropping his gun. The other man desperately tried to pull back now when it was way too late. In panic, he somersaulted backwards out of the saddle and over the horse's rump. The horse itself backed up with its powerful muscles and trampled him in its efforts to get free.

The man with his leg jammed was suddenly released and he fell sideways, striking his head against the rock.

There was pure hell behind the two riders. No one in the rest of the posse knew exactly what had happened and one man put his mount right up to the downed horse, trying to see. He retreated when Keel's next shot took his hat off.

Keel levered in another shell, the sound of the gunfire dying, and in the lull he heard the snarling scream of a cougar.

It came from the slopes of the hogback, and even as he snapped his head around to look, straining to see, for that slope was now in deep, creeping shadow as the sun sank lower, he heard a distant, almost soft *thud!*

He didn't realize what it was right away: he wanted to see that big cat, make sure where it was. Then he realized the cat's scream hadn't been one of triumph as they sometimes cut loose with after a kill, or even a threatening scream to scare away another animal after its meal.

That cat was in pain . . . and it was then he realized the distant *thud!* was a special kind of gunshot. A sound he had heard once before . . . *the day his seed bull had died!*

'McMann!'

Then there was more shooting from the posse. Someone had gotten down behind the dead horse blocking the trail, was raking the rim with rifle fire. Other men had clambered part-way up the walls and he was suddenly dodging flying rock chips and whining lead.

Keel cut loose with four fast shots, ricocheting his bullets from the walls. In the narrow gap, the lead whipped from one side to the other and a man yelped in fear as the ricochets slashed air close to him. The firing stopped as men hunted better cover and Keel smiled grimly as he emptied the rifle after them.

He took time to reload the magazine and by then the posse was scattering. He didn't aim to wait around and see what they were going to do.

The claybank was contentedly grazing on some grass behind the rocks where he had left it and didn't appreciate the way he dropped into the saddle from a rock above. It snorted and bucked a little but by then he had the reins and his heels kicked into its flanks. He swung the horse downslope, keeping the rocks between himself and the narrow neck where guns were still shooting and men were shouting confused orders to each other.

Deep shadows chilled him as he burst out on to the first slopes of the hogback and he instinctively looked around for signs of the big cat.

McMann's camp seemed deserted from this distance. Even if he had sent Joel Askins to go see if he had brought down the cougar, the man couldn't reach the hogback before Keel had crossed it. *He hoped!*

He hauled rein abruptly.

Two things — *three* — caught his attention. First it was a glimpse of the wounded cougar slinking over a ledge, moving very slowly, falteringly, the hind-quarters almost dragging on the ground. He swore: the animal was gut-shot! No hunter worthy of the name would let it go to die a long, suffering death. Even Indians didn't let animals suffer any longer than necessary: it was mighty bad medicine and did nothing to earn them honour, either in this world or the Spirit World that awaited every man.

'McMann and his goddamn long shots!' gritted Keel, wondering if he could get to the ledge in time to see the big cat and put it out of its misery. He doubted he would find it before full dark but set the claybank forward again — then saw the other two things that clenched his belly.

The naked Cole brothers, stretched back across boulders, side by side, both with gaping bullet wounds. He couldn't tell from here if the cougar had been feeding on them yet but there was no doubt in his mind that Andy and Tully Cole had been callously used as bait: no man deserved that.

A surge of fury like he had never known momentarily blinded him and he had even started to haul the claybank to the left, knowing that McMann had to be out there on the flats, but sanity prevailed. He could see the distant tents of the camp and wondered if McMann was training his glasses or telescopic sight on him right now . . .

He plunged the horse back into the shadows, wondering now how he was going to get across that open slope. If he rode forward, there was a good chance McMann could still be watching, looking for the wounded cougar, and if he saw Keel he would blow him out of the saddle with that big gun and Keel wouldn't even know what had hit him.

But if he stayed put, or tried to go back, he would run into the posse. And they were coming like a cavalry charge now: he could hear them thundering through the draw. He knew they had to be in Indian file because of its narrowness, but they would scatter as soon as they hit the slope and in this light there would be too many for him to handle.

He decided to make his dash across the open slope of the hogback, try to swing up near the ledge where the wounded cat had gone. There was a chance the cat was still crouched up there in the black shadows, licking its wounds, suffering, and in savage mood. It might, in a last desperate, instinctive gesture, leap down upon him or the horse as he passed underneath, so he had to turn more sharply, set the horse almost directly up the slope.

Which would mean it would slow down — and give the posse a target they could shoot at at their leisure.

How the hell had he gotten himself into such a mess?

No one to blame but himself and that sure wasn't going to help, he allowed, as he jumped the claybank forward and started his run across the open slope. The shadows were washing down the hogback now like a dark tide and he figured he would make a mighty hard target even for McMann's fancy sights.

In any case, he was committed now.

'There he goes!' shouted a voice behind him but he didn't bother looking around. He knew it had to be the first of the posse hitting the slope.

Guns hammered and he saw puffs of dust ahead, to his left — downslope — and only one on the right, upslope. Shooting *across* a slope could be just as hard and confusing as shooting downhill or uphill. Especially in this fast-fading light.

Keel crouched low and lashed the

racing horse with the rein ends, wheeling it suddenly directly up the grade. It protested but he felt it bunch its muscles under him and then respond.

At the same moment he realized the guns had stopped shooting at him.

This time he did look back over his shoulder — and almost hauled rein he was so shocked at what he saw.

The posse had stopped, bunched up again now, making a fine lot of targets if he wanted to get off a few shots. But they were oblivious to him.

They had found the Coles.

Keel slowed the horse this side of the approaches to the ledge where he had seen the big cat disappear. He glimpsed the cat's blood trail then, scattered patches that caught a little light and reflected redly. He figured the animal wouldn't last the night although he had known cougars to take a week to die from a gut-shot. He swore again at McMann's callousness, but he had himself to think about and, as he drew his Colt, watching the country mighty carefully, the horse walking now, blowing hard, someone called behind and below.

'Keel! Adam Keel!'

He stopped, then put the horse deeper into shadow before turning and looking down. The posse had dismounted and were gathered around the Coles' bodies on the boulders. Keel watched but didn't answer. The same voice called again and he recognized its owner as Blair Newman, a wrangler with Broken Rail, he had once fought to a standstill over the way the man was ill-treating one of his horses. He was a tough *hombre*, Blair Newman . . .

'Keel, you know anythin' about this? Andy and Tully?'

Keel still didn't answer.

'Looks to us like they been left for cougar bait — splashes of blood close to 'em down here and cougar tracks. He's wounded. Someone shot him I guess just before he pounced on the Coles.'

'McMann,' Keel said, calling just loud enough for them to hear.

The men, who had been murmuring amongst themselves went suddenly quiet.

'How you know that?' shouted one man, Reardon, a saloon lounger, Keel thought.

'Work it out. You can still just see his camp yonder. He's been itching to try out that new gun — mostly on me, but I figure he'd want to sight it in on a live target. So he set out the Coles, hoping to bring in the big cougar — which he did.'

That caused a slight stir. 'The *big* one?' Reardon asked.

'Yeah, saw him slinking over this here ledge. Gutshot. Blood everywhere . . . What you boys aiming to do?'

They went into a brief huddle and then Blair Newman said, 'No one had much use for Tully, but Andy weren't that bad. None too honest but who is? He was tough, but — well, we ain't happy about any man bein' just left for wild animals, stripped buck-nekked into the bargain. Looks like a crow's been at their eyes, too . . . '

'Get to your point, Blair.'

'Don't push it, Keel! We could blow you outa that saddle right now if we wanted to!'

'Some of you might manage it.'

'All right, all right. Listen, we ain't been paid what we was promised, and Askins has been hazin' us ragged. The married men want to get back to their families. So, Keel? You can go to hell, far as we're concerned. It's end of the trail for us. None of us wants to finish up like the Coles, not the way you been pickin' us off — an' you're headin' into that canyon country you know better'n anyone. We're callin' it quits. So don't start shootin'! We're all through here, savvy?'

Keel sat there, unmoving, gripping his six-gun, watching as the men mounted. The bodies had been wrapped in blankets and two men carried them over their saddles.

They turned and rode down on to the flat. Keel wondered if they were going to call in at McMann's camp. They might if they were riled enough, but they were pretty damn scared of McMann, too.

Anyway, why should he worry? If they were off his neck, that suited him fine. He lifted the reins and turned the skittish horse towards the ledge. The animal obviously sensed the cougar somewhere nearby and —

'You ain't going anywhere, Adam. Just leather that Colt and lift your hands slowly, OK?'

12

Prey

'Wondered when you'd show up, Joel,' Keel said, ramming the six-gun back into his holster.

'Mr McMann likes a man on the spot. He figured he'd winged the big cat and being the fine sportsman he is, sent me up to see if it was dead yet.' Askins snorted behind Keel. 'Found yellow and green in amongst the blood so I'd say he gutshot the pussy.'

'And is content to let it go — or let someone else track it down and finish it off. Yeah, some fine sportsman.' Keel turned his head and saw Askins standing on a rock above him covering him with one six-gun, the other still in leather. 'You've come down some since the days of the Border Patrol, Joel.'

'Well, a man was a fool taking all

those risks down there for a few dollars a month. Mr McMann pays more in a day than I could earn in weeks with the Patrol.'

He climbed down nimbly enough and stood beside the claybank, gesturing for Keel to dismount.

'Wouldn't say your life's exactly been a success, neither, Adam.'

'Aw, I dunno — I never did need much. Trouble is, what little I settled for, was taken from me by McMann. And I can't let him get away with that.'

'Come on — get down! No, I savvy you pretty well. I know you're after McMann, but I can't let you get to him. That's why he pays me.'

'Bit of a bind, then, ain't it?' Keel said swinging his leg over the horse and jumping down. But he pushed off the claybank and instead of letting his leg fall straight down beside the other, swung it against Askins' gunhand.

The Mescalero moccasin connected with the gun and Askins staggered as it fell. Keel slugged him even as the man reached for his second Colt. Askins stumbled to hands and knees and Keel kicked the gun away and drove another kick into his side. Askins rolled, grunting, snatching up a handful of gravel and tossing it at Keel's head as the fugitive closed in.

Keel jerked his head aside, the gravel missing, but it gave Askins a chance to lunge to his feet and he came in with head lowered and arms spread. His head rammed Keel in the midriff and the arms closed about him, carrying him over backwards. Locked together they rolled down the slope, punching and kicking, trying to ram knees into each other. They hit the flat and brought up short against the base of a boulder. Keel writhed free, kicked both feet into Askins' snarling face just as the man launched himself in a dive.

Keel rolled but Askins' flailing body fell on him and pinned his legs. Joel was fast and well versed in rough-and-tumble fighting. He wrenched around and up, lifted an elbow and dropped

215

down with all his weight into Keel's midriff. The man gagged and felt the world tilt as bright lights whirled behind his eyes. His ears roared and his throat burned as he fought for breath.

Askins straddled him and punched him in the face, two heavy blows. Keel slumped and Askins hit him again for good measure. Panting, he looked down at the man and then swung free and started to stand up.

Keel came to life, swept his leg around, bringing Askins down again. He flung himself across the surprised hardcase, grabbed the man by the ears, and slammed his head against the ground. Joel's eyes crossed and Keel slammed his head again, hooked him under the jaw. Joel shook his head and snapped his upper body forward, driving his head into Keel's face. Blood spurted from Keel's nose and he lurched upright. Askins kicked free, swung a boot into Keel and, as the man sprawled, turned and lunged up the slope to where one of his six-guns glinted in the last rays of the sun.

Keel was dazed, wiped blood from his face, blinking rapidly to get back his focus. Askins dived on his six-gun and whipped on to his back, shooting even as Keel drew his own gun in a blur of speed.

The shots blended into one crashing roar that bounced off the rocks around them.

When the gunsmoke cleared a little, Keel was still standing, feet spread, gun cocked and ready for another shot. Askins was huddled on his side, his gun on the ground, face screwed up in pain. There was blood oozing through his fingers where he clamped them against his side, just under his lower ribs.

'Damn — you, Adam!' he gritted. 'You sure — ain't slowed — down any!'

'And you're just as sneaky as always . . . You hit bad?'

'Bad enough. You better finish it!'

Keel arched his eyebrows, wiping blood from his dripping nose again as he slowly climbed the slope to where the hardcase lay. He holstered the gun, knelt and pulled the man's hands away from the wound with an effort.

'Hard to see in this light — but you'll be OK when you get to a sawbones.'

He was surprised to hear Askins try to laugh, a *bitter*-sounding laugh.

'You're joking! I can't go — anywhere! Christ, you dunno McMann. He don't mess with losers.'

'McMann? What the hell's happened to you, Joel? He's only another man, a mite richer than most — all right! A *helluva* lot richer than most folk, but that don't make him God.'

'Near — enough.' Askins shook his head, lips drawn back in a rictus of pain. 'I got a sister — in Laredo. He can't get to me — direct — he'll get to me through her! No, Adam, I ain't gonna get to any sawbones — and you ain't taking me down to McMann.'

Keel stood looking down at the wounded man for a long moment, frowning a little.

'OK — How about *you* take *me* down?'

★ ★ ★

McMann waved away Andre as the French cook offered him some more dessert from the silver dish. The rich man dabbed at his lips with a napkin.

'*Merci, Andre — Tres bon!*'

Andre gave a little bow and retreated from the tent and McMann sat back in his canvas chair, reaching for a cigar. Then the chef appeared again, looking perturbed. He spoke rapidly in French, a trace of alarm in his voice.

McMann frowned, got quickly out of the chair and picked up his gold-capped shooting stick which was never far from his hand. The chef hurried away again as McMann stepped outside and looked into the dusk, the sky writhing like a nest of crimson and gold snakes with a trace of glowing blue in between. Soon it would be full dark.

But for now there was enough light

for him to see two horsemen approaching, one slightly ahead of the second who seemed to be slumped over a little. McMann thumbed-off the button safety catch on the gold cap and strained to make out the newcomers.

A smile spread slowly across his face as he recognized Adam Keel in front, his hands roped to the saddle horn. The second rider was Joel Askins, holding a six-gun and covering Keel. The bodyguard seemed to have been injured but McMann gave *that* no further thought.

'Well, this is a pleasant surprise! Something that assures me of a good night's sleep — a *very* good night's sleep, I should say! Good work, Joel!'

The riders came slowly across the cleared camp ground to within a few yards of the tent. Askins gestured to Keel.

'You can get down now.'

McMann tensed, started to speak, reminding Askins that Keel's hands were roped to the saddle horn, but it was too late. The ropes fell away and

Keel swung down and slapped aside the gunstick as McMann desperately brought it up.

He grabbed the man's wrist, pulled him in close and punched him in the mid-section. McMann staggered, his eyes bulging as he fought to keep down the fine French cooking he had just eaten. Keel took the gunstick and flung it away and hit McMann in the face, putting him down on his back.

'Joel!' McMann screeched. *'Shoot him, you fool!'*

Askins lined-up his Colt on Keel and pulled the trigger. There was nothing but a cold *click*!

Joel shrugged and dropped the empty gun back into his holster. Only then did McMann notice there were no cartridges in the belt loops.

His face, red and smeared with a little blood from Keel's blow, turned mighty ugly. 'You let him get the better of you!'

He scrambled to his feet and Askins nodded wearily, holding a hand to his wounded side which had been roughly bandaged with one of his spare shirts by Keel before they had left the hogback. He glanced at Keel.

'Maybe we'll meet again one day, Adam.'

'Could be . . . *Adios*, Joel.'

Askins nodded and looked at McMann. 'I'm quitting, boss. I'll collect what gear I've left in the Pullman and then I'm riding out. Can't say I've enjoyed working for you, but you pay well. Still, money ain't everythin', I guess.'

He turned his horse and rode away into the gathering darkness.

'No one walks out on me!' McMann yelled after him. 'Don't think I'll let you get away with this, Joel! And if you see that whore in San Antone, tell her I haven't finished with her yet, either!'

Askins rode on without reply or looking back.

McMann was breathing heavily and he turned to Keel, no fear showing openly, but there was a wariness in his eyes.

'I should've let them kill you long ago!'

'Would've been to your advantage,' Keel agreed readily. 'Not to mine though. Well, McMann, just what the hell am I going to do with a miserable snake like you? I'm open to ideas — any suggestions?'

McMann took in a deep, steadying breath as he held a silk kerchief to his bleeding mouth.

'Perhaps we could talk about it over a glass of Napoleon brandy — the genuine article, I can assure you.'

'Yeah, that sounds like a good idea . . . '

Keel dropped an arm across McMann's shoulders and they started back into the tent.

'If it's simply a matter of compensation . . . ' McMann said tentatively as they went through the flap doorway.

★ ★ ★

Adam Keel entered San Antone from the east, coming in by the mean back streets with the rising sun behind him.

He had taken time to trim his hair and have a rough shave with the Mescalero's scalping knife, taking off the frontier moustache he had worn for so many years. Askins had given him another of his spare shirts from his saddle-bags and with a pair of McMann's handmade South American riding boots, he looked pretty damn fine, he reckoned.

It wasn't likely that folk would recognize him right off, though a second — or maybe a third — look would identify him. But that was OK. He didn't need a lot of time here.

His main problem was to find the girl.

He knew that if she had walked out on McMann she wouldn't have any money and that made it harder to figure out where she might be staying. He checked out the Pullman first and there were signs it had been searched hurriedly and he wondered if Joel Askins had done this, or had the girl decided to look for money herself? She would no doubt know where McMann kept any cash.

So she might be staying in a hotel after all.

There was really only one 'good' hotel in San Antone, and that was the Del Sol which fronted the plaza. Not the kind of place where Keel could hope to go and not be noticed, but there were ways and means.

For one thing, he was on pretty good terms with Angelo, one of the servants who worked in the kitchen. So he tethered the claybank in a patch of grass in a vacant lot behind the Del Sol and made his way to the rear door.

A blousy Mexican woman came out with a dish of soapy water and tossed it into the alley, starting when she saw him, gasping as she hurriedly crossed herself, dark eyes bulging.

'It's all right, Maria — it's Keel. OK?'

She stared, still ready to run like a

spooked doe. 'Ah, Keel! The posse say you are dead!'

'Here in the flesh, Maria — send Angelo out, OK?'

She half-smiled, hesitated, then went back inside and a few minutes later a skinny, yet handsome, young Mexican appeared.

'*Buenas dias*, Señor Keel. You take a risk coming here.'

'So I won't waste time, Angelo. I'm looking for the rich man's woman, Señorita Lorrance, she staying here?'

'*Si*, she in room nine. Ah, now *there* is a *muy bueno* woman, eh?'

'Yeah, she's a looker. Can you get her down here?'

Angelo's smile disappeared. 'I don' think she's awake yet.'

'You go wake her then — here.' He took a silver coin from his pocket — courtesy of Shelby McMann — and handed it to the boy.

'No, no, *dinero* don' matter, *señor* — but waking the *señorita* so early!'

'It's important, *amigo*. Mighty important.'

Angelo nodded. 'I go.'

Keel had to cool his heels for fifteen minutes, before the girl appeared, fully dressed and looking beautiful in the early sunlight. But she didn't seem all that happy as she looked around for Keel and he stepped out from behind a pile of crates.

'You're the last person I expected to see.'

'I guess so. You seen Joel Askins?'

Her cool gaze studied him as she nodded slowly. 'We met last night. He'd been to a doctor to have a wound in his side attended to. A wound he said you gave him . . .'

'He's OK then?' She nodded and he added, 'Did he tell you that McMann said he was coming after you for walking out on him?'

Her face paled and she lost some of the confidence. Her gloved hands tightened on the straps of the small handbag she held.

'He mentioned it.' Her voice was low and he knew she was deeply afraid and trying not to let it show.

'Yeah, McMann's a mean snake, all right. You find any money in the Pullman?'

Her look was up-from-under. 'The Pullman rail car you mean? I haven't been there.'

'Not even to collect some of the high-fashion clothes you wear? You'd be able to sell them for a good deal anywhere west of the Mississippi. There's a kind of high society out here amongst the cattlemen and business-men and their wives would kill to get their hands on a Paris gown, even if there wasn't anywhere they could really wear it.'

'All right. Yes, I took the clothes! He bought them for me. He gave me nothing else but clothes and a little jewellery, but he kept that locked away.'

'With his ready cash.'

'Yes. He had it in a brassbound chest bolted to the floor in the bedroom.'

'It was busted open when I saw it. If

it wasn't you, likely it was Askins. He left town?'

'He said he was going after he had a little sleep. He did seem in something of a hurry, now I think about it, but he took time to come and see Judge Michaels with me.'

Keel frowned. 'What'd he want to see the judge for? For that matter, why did you?'

She paused before answering. 'Joel and I had certain information that never came to light at your trial. How McMann bribed witnesses and the jury as well as Tully Cole.'

'Hell, everyone knew that, even Judge Michaels, but there was no way of proving it — '

'The judge has statutory declarations from Joel and myself that McMann did buy the jurors — through his attorney, of course, but the corruption was there. And while you did some of the things you were charged with, in themselves they would not have earned you such a long sentence on the Three Creeks chain gang. The *witnesses* exaggerated unduly . . . '

Keel wasn't sure where this was going now. 'I know that . . . even Michaels knew it but he was bound by law to give me the sentence to fit the crimes the jury convicted me of.'

'Yes, he said that — but now he has our statements he's going to quash the rest of your sentence. Whatever time you've served will be enough for the assault charges which are the only ones you should have been tried for.'

He stared at her blankly.

'In other words, Adam Keel, you're a free man.'

He was too stunned to speak for a while. His astonishment brought a slow smile to her lips.

'Yes, it *was* a nice gesture on the part of Joel and myself, Keel. No need to thank us . . . '

Keel stirred himself. 'Hell, I *do* thank you. I-I'm just so damn surprised. Now why in hell would you and Askins do a thing like that for me?'

She shrugged. 'McMann's a master at giving people a raw deal, myself included. I thought you'd received one, too, but most of all, you are the *only* man I've ever known to not only stand up to McMann, but to throw him into a fit at the mere mention of your name. And I *know* he was afraid of you, deep down, despite all his money and power. I just felt a man who could do that to him didn't deserve to be a fugitive for the rest of his life. He'd have put a bounty on your head if he couldn't reach you himself, you know.'

'Maybe you're right — Joel surprises me, too. We were never what you might call pards in the Border Patrol, but we got along OK.'

'Joel respected you, Keel. He told me so. He was feeling a little bad about selling out to McMann and that was brought on by you holding out against all odds and — then doctoring him after you shot him and giving him a chance to get away.'

'Well, I'll be damned. Have to buy

him a drink if I ever see him again . . . '

'You'll have to go and see Judge Michaels and make everything official.'

'Be happy to.'

'Then what . . . ?'

'Well, somehow me and folks around here never did get on too well, but I like it out at Anchor Basin. Reckon I'll rebuild. Owe it to old Stew in a way . . . '

'I think I can see what you mean.' Then her smile broadened and she placed a hand on his forearm. 'I wish you luck . . . you stubborn man!'

'And where are you headed?' he asked, smiling back.

She sobered, sighed and shrugged. 'Thought I might go to Austin. I have a little money left.' The way she said it made him wonder if it had been Askins who had pried open that brassbound chest after all. 'Not much, but I think I can sell off those Paris fashions better there. There is a quite large social set there, it being the capital, and with all those politicians and their wing-dings . . . '

He smiled. 'You'll land on your feet.'

Her eyes snapped at him. 'If you mean some senator will make me his consort.'

Keel held up a hand swiftly. 'Sorry. Didn't mean to insult you.'

'I take a lot of insulting, Keel, but — not from you. Anyway, I thought after I sell the clothes I might even come back here, see how you're getting along with the rebuilding of your ranch.'

He had gone very still. 'Why?'

She smiled. 'Can't think of anyone I'd rather have as a — bodyguard. You *did* say McMann had threatened to come after me . . . '

'Yeah, well, I guess I could . . . take care of you. But you don't have to worry about McMann.'

She frowned. 'Why?'

'He's busy. Looking for that big mountain cat he wounded in the canyon country out there. I showed him the way in. But it was dark — I doubt he'll be able to find his way out again in a hurry . . .'

She hooked an arm through his. 'I knew he had underestimated you — but not just how badly! And you really didn't need to come here now, did you?'

He shrugged. 'C'mon, I'll buy you breakfast.'

He knew it wouldn't last, of course, but — well, hell, she was sure a looker . . .

★   ★   ★

Shelby McMann had never been so afraid in all of his pampered life.

It had been bad enough being brought in here by that bastard Keel in the darkness, *dragged* along behind the man's horse, stumbling and falling in the night over the broken ground.

The sounds of the night animals had set his heart hammering wildly and twice he had heard the scream of a cougar.

'That's yours, McMann,' Keel had said casually. 'The one that's still carrying your lead in his guts — or maybe it went right on through, but it sure busted him up on the way.'

'How — how can you tell?'

'That cat's hurting. You can hear it in his cry. You're a lousy hunter, McMann, had it too soft. A man wounds an animal, he's duty-bound to go after it, track it down as quick as he can and put it out of its misery. A man who won't do that is no man at all . . . which kind of suits you, don't it?'

'You son of a bitch! You won't get away with this! I'll see *you're* hunted down and put out of *your* misery!'

'Have at it, McMann — you're welcome to try.'

McMann's trousers were torn at the knees. The rope around his wrists hurt, and his breath was rasping in his throat. Along the way, he had lost the fine meal Andre had cooked him and he was hungry now despite his fear.

Keel must have had eyes like a cat,

the way he rode in this broken canyon country. The horse seemed to instinctively pick its way but now and again, Keel nudged him the way *he* wanted him to go.

McMann suddenly thought about the stars, clear and crisp in the Texas sky above. But what was the use? He didn't know how to find direction by stars or any other natural feature — he had always *bought* that kind of thing when he needed it, paid someone to do it for him.

Now he wished he had paid attention when some of those dirty, rough-voiced frontiersmen, who had led him on many a hunt for game — all taken with long shots — had talked amongst themselves within his hearing, talked about the secrets of navigating by natural signs.

It must have been near midnight when Keel had finally stopped, climbed down out of the saddle and walked back to where the sweating, gasping McMann had flopped down onto the nearest rock. One stroke from the Indian knife Keel wore on his belt and McMann's hands were free — and then he discovered the tingling, painful pleasure of once again having circulation back in his lower arms and hands.

'Well, here we are, McMann. Nice little natural amphitheatre surrounded by rock walls and plenty of ledges. Even a little water-hole yonder — but you'll have time to look for that yourself. Give you something to do.'

'Wha — what the *hell* are you playing at Keel?'

'It's no game, McMann. This isn't something you can call off when you feel like it. And you sure as hell can't buy your way out.'

'Out of *what* for Chris'sakes?'

Keel smiled in the darkness. McMann couldn't see it but if he had been able to, it would have chilled his blood.

'Out of your obligations. I told you: you wound an animal, you just don't let it crawl away to die in agony: you go

237

after it and do the right thing — put it out of its misery.'

'You're — mad!' McMann's voice cracked. 'I — I'm not even armed!'

'I thought of that — but I'll fix that before I go and I'm going now.'

'No, wait!' McMann ran at the claybank as Keel started it forward, clawing at Keel's leg. 'Don't go! Don't leave me here! You mentioned money. Look, you don't know just how much I have! Millions in assets. I can lay my hands on hundreds of thousands immediately. Does that figure give you pause? Say a hundred thousand dollars?'

'How about two hundred thousand?'

'All right! Is that your price? It's yours, I give you my word . . . just get me out of here.'

Keel kicked him away coldly and McMann sprawled on the rocks. Keel took a six-gun he had taken from one of the posse men he had killed and threw it near the man.

'I'll leave six cartridges on that rock

yonder as I go by . . . they won't cost you a red cent.'

'No! *Don't leave me!*'

But Keel was riding away, paused at the rock he had indicated and left the six cartridges there.

McMann was staggering to his feet, picking up the empty six-gun as Keel rode away into the darkness. He triggered it anyway, in towering frustration, just to make sure, but, of course, the hammer fell on empty chambers. Sobbing, he stumbled to the rock, scooped up the cartridges, dropping two irretrievably down a deep crevice as he fumbled the rest into the Colt's cylinder.

Panting now, eyes white with panic, he ran to the foot of the trail Keel had taken and fired wildly, cursing hysterically. Only after the echoes were dying did he realize he had totally emptied the weapon. *Now he had no protection at all!*

He groped his way to the rock and slumped down on it, hands between his shaking knees, staring dully at the barely seen rock between his feet.

He must have dozed a little for when he looked up, starting, it was just showing daylight, outlining the rimrock and spilling down into the amphitheatre. He was hungry and mighty thirsty. Keel had told him there was a water-hole. He looked around quickly, hurried in the direction Keel had pointed out and amongst the big boulders that would be shaded by the rimrock during the day, he found the small water-hole.

He wanted to shout in his triumph, but his throat was far too dry for that. McMann dropped full length, plunged his face into the chill water and drank deeply, greedily. Gasping, slobbering, he lay there, stretched out, face only inches above the surface as the ripples flattened out.

Then he heard a small clatter of stones behind him and something moved as it was reflected in the water . . .

He twisted onto his back, face

terror-stricken now, feeling the water he had gulped down surging back up into his throat.

On the ledge above crouched the big cougar, tawny flanks and belly splashed with dried blood, more still oozing from the belly wound. It looked like part of the animal's intestines were hanging out, touching the rough rock. The huge, wounded cat was fever-ridden, parched with thirst — and now there was a man between it and the water it craved so urgently . . .

The cat snarled, baring massive, curved ivory fangs, yellow eyes watching the terrified man below as he scrabbled frantically backwards, vomiting water in his fear.

The cougar knew it was dying and one final surge of hatred for this two-legged being that had brought about its present situation was enough to bunch its steel muscles one last time.

With a high-pitched scream that rang from the rimrock, the big cat leaped.

We do hope that you have enjoyed reading this large print book.

Did you know that all of our titles are available for purchase?

We publish a wide range of high quality large print books including:
Romances, Mysteries, Classics
General Fiction
Non Fiction and Westerns

Special interest titles available in large print are:
The Little Oxford Dictionary
Music Book, Song Book
Hymn Book, Service Book

Also available from us courtesy of Oxford University Press:
Young Readers' Dictionary
(large print edition)
Young Readers' Thesaurus
(large print edition)

For further information or a free brochure, please contact us at:
Ulverscroft Large Print Books Ltd.,
The Green, Bradgate Road, Anstey,
Leicester, LE7 7FU, England.
Tel: (00 44) **0116 236 4325**
Fax: (00 44) **0116 234 0205**